The Rats of Wolfe Island

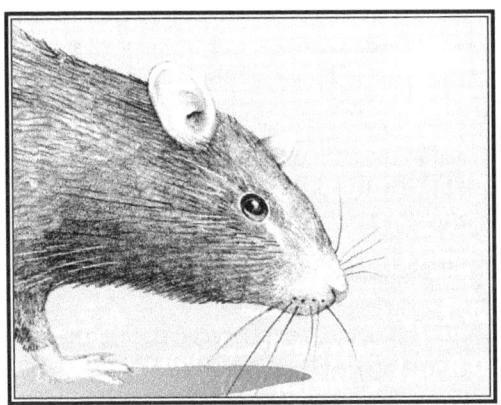

ALAN HORSFIELD

EJH
TALENT
PROMOTION

First published in 2002 by Lothian Press

Copyright © Alan Horsfield 2002

This edition published in 2016 by EJH Talent Promotion

The right of Alan Horsfield to be identified as the author of this work has been asserted under the *Copyright Amendment (Moral Rights) Act 2000.*

Requests and enquiries should be addressed to:
Alan Horsfield, 9 Milman Drive, Craiglie QLD 4877
anehorsfield@westnet.com.au

National Library of Australia Cataloguing-in-Publication data:

Creator:	Horsfield, Alan, author.
Title:	The rats of Wolfe Island / Alan Horsfield.
ISBN:	9780994457967 (paperback)
	9780646909943 (ebook)
Target Audience:	For young adults.
Subjects:	Rats – Effect of radiation on – Fiction.
	Animal experimentation – Fiction.
Dewey Number:	A823.3

Cover illustration by David Dickson
Design and layout by DiZign Pty Ltd, Sydney

Printed in Australia

Acknowledgements

My thanks to Dr Wolfgang Pfaeltzer and his wife Doreen, of Savasi Island, Savusavu, Fiji Islands, for allowing me to use their small island as the setting for this work of fiction.

Thanks also to my wife Elaine for her suggestions and many proofreadings.

My apologies to our cat, Macavity, for putting him through these fictional ordeals.

Chapter 1

The email was puzzling. No, it was confusing.

I took it from the pocket of my denim jacket and re-read the terrible typing.

It was more than just the typing. It looked as if it had been written by someone not fully coherent, or as if it had somehow been badly copied.

> To: EddyHaite@iserve.com
> From: king@iserve.com
> Subject: Experement finshed
>
> Eddy„ hi
>
> Just to letting you know I have made stop to the experiments, as you suggested. It was not achieving nothing much. The subjects were not making the kind of progres I have hoped. They were not getting smarter and I was growing old and wasting our time.
>
> Please tyo tell you this. Don't
>
> comeback.There is no need to come and visit me as I will be closing the lab down and I will sit on my verandah

1

and watch the sut set with a nice cool
drink> >

All I can say thank god its over

Rex king

(king of Wolfe island.

Not the Kingy style at all. Something was disturbingly amiss. I sighed deeply, then realised that I was standing in the middle of the road.

I looked in each direction, not really expecting to see anything more than a deserted road under a canopy of lush green.

The rattling bus that had transported me to this isolated part of the coast had disappeared in a cloud of dust and diesel fumes.

I crossed the corrugated road and dropped down onto a narrow beach. Wolfe Island was just across the lagoon. This was my third trip to the island. My first visit had been filled with anticipation and excitement, but now all I felt was apprehension and caution. I hardly noticed the tall, swaying palms and the clear skies.

I looked up and down the beach. For a moment I had the feeling that I was being watched. The feeling passed and all I felt was foolish.

I untied the little rowboat that was half-hidden under some beach foliage, found the oars a little bit further into the scrub where I had hidden them, and prepared for my short trip across the shallow coral waters to Wolfe Island. I bailed out some old rainwater that had collected in the boat since my last trip a month or so earlier before dropping my backpack into the bow.

Kingy's rowboat wasn't anywhere to be seen. That made sense. He would be on Wolfe Island.

My mind wasn't on the rowing. I don't really like rowing but it was the most convenient way to cross the couple of hundred metres to the island. Wading through the shallows at low tide would have been OK except for the narrow tidal channel right in the middle, which separated Wolfe Island from the main island. I struggled to set the boat on course for the opposite beach. It was only when the boat freed itself from the gritty sand that I started to relax a little and could survey the shoreline I had just left.

Behind the strip of vegetation was 'the road'. The coral-based track up the coast from the main small town could hardly be called a road but it was the only way to get around the island unless you had a powerful motor boat. I could still see the narrow single-lane wooden bridge that I had just crossed before alighting from the local bus.

The road appeared totally deserted, but I wouldn't have been surprised if someone had stepped out of the bushes and watched as I crossed the channel. It was uncanny how someone could suddenly appear.

All evidence of the bus's existence had quickly vanished. No rumbling, no black exhaust fumes, no cloud of fine dust.

We had hardly passed another vehicle on our trip out from town. This was well away from any tourist track. And this time I wasn't a tourist.

This was about as remote as you could get without finding your own sandy atoll somewhere out in the ocean beyond the horizon. The ocean here looks as if it goes on forever.

Briefly, almost enviously, I wondered what my uni friends might be doing at that moment. The first-year soccer team would be at training. That I knew for sure.

A slight movement caught my eye just as I was about to prepare myself for the short haul to the island. Just above the high water mark but still on the sand, under the overhang of some mangroves, was an animal. At first I thought it was a small, dark dog—maybe a pup—but there were no dogs on this island. I didn't think there were any feral cats. There were no native furry animals as far as I knew. But this was definitely a furry little creature.

As it moved slowly back into the shadows of the overhang I realised that it was a rather large rat. And it was watching me very intently. It hadn't ducked for cover when it realised that it had been seen but merely moved to a less conspicuous hide to watch me.

'Bloody rat!' I swore softly.

It was disturbing, quite disturbing, knowing what I knew about Kingy's experiments.

I wiped my brow on my sleeve, then took the oars and started pulling. It should have been a perfect day. The sky was clear. The water was crystal clear. I could see small blue iridescent fish darting for safety as the boat moved over their coral habitats. Tropical birds could be heard in the deep green forest of the island.

It was a scene of peace and tranquillity.

I could have been the only person around for miles and miles—except for Rex King. The thought brought me back to reality. Rex King, who I hoped to see very shortly and who had given up his experiments partly because of my advice.

I reached the channel and prepared to haul a little harder on the oars to avoid being pulled off course by the current, but it must have been full high tide because the current wasn't running. The little boat slipped easily over the channel and was soon grinding into the gravel of the small beach.

A narrow track led through the dim vegetation to Kingy's house and lab on the seaward side of the island.

I secured the boat with an old bit of fading nylon rope. It was then that I noticed that Kingy's boat was not in its usual place beside the track. It didn't seem all that important at that moment.

I grabbed my backpack, slung it onto my back and set off through the trees. I became aware of a rustling sound in the undergrowth. It sounded like something was scrambling through the leaf litter, keeping pace with me.

I thought it might be Kingy's old cat checking me out. I tentatively called in the general direction of the sound. 'Hey, Macavity, it's me!'

The rustling stopped suddenly, which did nothing to dispel the sense of fore-boding.

What was once tranquil and beautiful now seemed shadowy and forbidding. Peace had become isolation. The island that

Kingy called a tropical haven was more like the prison of Devil's Island.

I started to sweat. I hoped it was from the humidity.

I reached over to my backpack and took out a small water bottle. After a gulp of water I replaced the almost depleted bottle and hurried on, hoping to leave the rustling and my wild thoughts behind.

Chapter 2

I met Rex on my first visit to the main island. I had only just started at uni and was making the most of my first mid-semester break. I should have been at home catching up on a science assignment, but I was prepared to bluff my way through it—or at least, get an extension of time to 'finish' it. I wasn't about to give up my holiday. I was off to wander around the Pacific—as cheaply as possible, much to my parents' chagrin.

I had just gone into a small wharfside café looking for something cheap and local to eat. The place was more or less empty. Rex was sitting in a far corner obviously enjoying a plate of fish and chips. I hardly noticed him, being more taken in by such an impressive café being located in such a small tropical town. It was better than any coffee shop on campus.

While waiting to be served I sat at one of the round tables adjacent to the large glassless windows. The cool, salty breeze drifted across the bay. I shut my eyes and let it massage my hot forehead. As a back-packer one tends to do a lot of walking, often in the tropical heat. The locals seem to know better.

He spoke first. 'Mad dogs and English-men.'

'I know. Go out in the midday sun,'

I answered not opening my eyes. 'But I'm more the Australian variety.'

'Where you heading?' he asked after stuffing a few more chips into his mouth.

'Thought I might explore this place—the island more than just the town. I'm actually looking for excuses not to make any serious decisions about uni until I return.'

'Procrastinating. A luxury of youth,' he said with a sigh. Then he added, 'Uni could be better than sleeping on some mosquito-infested beach in the middle of a downpour. And no way of finding a dry bed for at least twelve hours. That's when you'll realise that uni isn't all that bad.'

I shrugged and nodded, but I wasn't convinced. It was a bright sunny day and uni had been left far behind in the suburban smog. Right now uni could have been on the moon!

'It has its moments, I guess.' I rambled on about some of the things I liked.

He seemed interested in what I had to say. I gave my biased opinion of what I thought of unis, lecturers and uni traditions in general.

'Sometimes it's not a bad thing to have time off between school and university. Gives one a chance to grow up,' he mused.

'Dad'd prefer I used it to earn some money!' I countered.

He was amused. 'Ever done any lab work?' He tugged gently at a red scarf he had knotted around his neck.

'Sure. Done a bit of science. Like to try a bit of biology. Thought I might have a go at marine biology later on.'

As my meal arrived he came over and joined me at my table. He offered me his hand. 'King. Rex King. Or Kingy for short. Might be able to help you. And you might be able to help me.'

'Eddy Haite,' I said, 'H-A-I-T-E.'

He motioned me to start eating. As I ate he told me a bit about himself.

'I'm actually a research scientist, just up the coast from here.' He waited for a reaction, so I raised my eyebrows.

He then went on to explain how he had somehow been connected with investigations into the long-term effects of nuclear radiation on some of the less directly affected Pacific atolls and islands.

'Bikini?' I asked. It was the only island I could think of that had been bombed with atomic bombs.

He shook his head and continued to describe how he had spent quite a lot of time collecting samples and data. On one island he had found a small colony of rats that adapted very quickly to their changed environment. What had really attracted Kingy's attention was that the rats seemed to have undergone some genetic change. According to Kingy's observations they seemed to have developed advanced social behaviours.

I looked at him questioningly. The only word I could think of was 'mutants'. It came more from an old kid's TV cartoon about turtles than from scientific research.

He folded his arms, leaned back in his chair and gazed out across the water for a few moments before continuing. 'It was a bit hard to recognise at first. I didn't really expect anything, so I wasn't really looking in the right direction. When I did start looking it was obvious that their social hierarchy was more refined—certain rats had certain tasks. There seemed to be leaders, soldiers, workers …'

'Sounds like a bee hive!' I said.

He shrugged. 'That's almost too much of a simplification. Some had developed an 'I am superior' type attitude.'

Rats with attitude! Now that's something, I thought.

Rex continued, 'They used to watch our research team as we came and left the island. In the beginning they were observing us more closely than we were observing them.'

Rex explained that after several visits to one particular atoll he was convinced that the rats were more intelligent than your normal bush rat or sewer rat. He wasn't sure if it was a side-effect of the atomic tests in the east or some process of natural selection and evolution. The Galapagos weren't all that far away—as the tortoise crawls! It might even have been dietary—it might have been possible that the vegetation had developed some abnormal properties.

After a comprehensive report, a United Nations organisation picked up the information and offered him a grant to further his studies of the rats. The proviso was that he had to arrange a suitable location.

That's how he had come to this part of the world. The small national government was keen to be seen as part of the world science scene. They were also keen on getting project money spent in their country from such an august body.

'Knowing a few local politicians was also a help,' he added with a laugh.

He waved to a waitress to bring him some water and took some tablets from his loosely woven shoulder bag.

When the water arrived he popped the tablets in his mouth and downed them with a gulp of water. He massaged his forehead with his fingertips for a few moments.

Then he popped his proposal. 'I need a reliable lab assistant. Interested?'

I had just finished eating, but I didn't look up immediately.

'Great conditions. Free board, bunk by an open window, cold showers—when you remember to pump the water— no pay, unlimited supply of exotic island food and a chance to show me what you know!'

I pressed my thumb against my top front teeth, trying to show I was giving it serious consideration. My heart was racing with anticipation.

'Of course, all the fishing you can do in your spare time, a small private beach that will be yours—and mine— exclusively. No international hotel could offer that!' he grinned and I think he knew I was hooked.

'Trouble is you'd be on duty more or less all day every day. But the workload isn't onerous. There'll be ample time to relax.'

I was about to say I'd think about it when I realised that I was just playing games. 'Count me in!' I said with a broad grin. I could tell my science lecturer I was getting practical work experience!

He shook my hand vigorously. 'Now you'll see real island life. You're hired!'

I widened my eyes as I made a voiceless wow, then said with exaggerated formality, 'Thanks, Rex!'

'First job, call me Kingy. Then help me grab some of those supplies, and then we'll be off to the bus station—if you can call a bare patch of earth a bus station. The last bus goes in half an hour ...' he paused for effect, 'or sooner. Or later. And it's the only bus for at least two days!'

Chapter 3

The bus, an old Leyland, had windows but no glass. The dust from the road and the diesel fumes were sucked in every time the vehicle exceeded 40 kilometres per hour, which wasn't very often.

The discomfort meant nothing to me. I was fascinated by the changing landscape. The further we went the narrower the road became. Branches and palm fronds spread right across the road at times, turning it into a lush tunnel.

At other times the road ran right along the shoreline. The outer reef was plainly visible as the waves crashed just a few hundred metres off-shore, their white caps brilliant against the deep blue of the sea.

For a while Kingy was quiet. I think he was letting me enjoy myself. Finally he started talking about his rats.

'You know,' he said, 'when I went to collect the rats for the experiments I thought I was going to have one hell of a job getting them. Funny thing was, they were wary of me but it was as if they were willing—but not too willing—to be caught. They didn't try all that hard to escape, like it was a token effort just to keep me happy. It did make my life easier. I didn't want to stay on that rat-infested place too long! There was something definitely spooky about that place.'

I had no reply.

'Rats don't worry you?' he queried.

'Wouldn't be here if they did! I've cut up a few in my time.' I wasn't sure I was being entirely honest—rats locked up are not at all like rats roaming free.

'Won't be too much cutting up. Just keeping records and observing their behaviour. Sounds dull. Maybe it is for some people, but I get some sort of satisfaction out of making the occasional discovery, no matter how small. And it keeps the sponsors happy.'

As we rattled along we passed the occasional narrow, rutted track running off into the jungle, usually with a strip of low vegetation down the centre.

Kingy would say something like, 'Small village up there.'

I never saw any signs of village life except the rare, crude, vacant bus shelters that were at the junction of the tracks and main road. They seemed to be of standard design: four bush posts of different sizes and angles and a rusty corrugated iron roof.

At one point Kingy passed a comment on such a structure: 'Popular design, but it wouldn't survive a cyclone.'

'Maybe they know the local building inspector,' I joked.

Then we passed a track that was actually signposted 'Buka Buka Village'. The tired post leaned over dramatically and the deteriorating sign pointed more to a nearby log than along the track. The track appeared to have been used a bit more than the others we had seen.

'Must be an important village,' I observed flippantly.

'They think they are,' Kingy growled quietly without looking at me. He was silent for a while and I thought that I had said something to upset him.

Shortly afterwards the bus emerged from a stand of vine-draped tropical trees and rattled across a one-lane bridge. I swear the damn thing swayed.

'Wolfe Island,' Kingy said, nodding his head in the direction of a small coastal island. 'This is where we leave the comfort of Island Bus Services and take a short sea trip to the exclusive resort of King's Hideaway!'

The island was the stuff of picture postcards. Just across the sparking blue water I could see a couple of small secluded beaches and a mass of palm trees protruding above the general vegetation.

Could be paradise, I thought.

Chapter 4

The bus slowly grated to a stop. Kingy rose from his seat.

'Looks real good to me,' I said, following him down the aisle as the bus gave a final shudder before stopping. I wondered if it was a death rattle.

We alighted and retrieved our belongings from the under-carriage, a long external compartment below the seats, completely exposed to the elements. I only had one backpack, but Kingy had a month's supply of goods: cartons of pretty ordinary food, tins of fuel, some basic hardware and what looked like a carton of toilet paper. It was all coated in fine dust.

Kingy thumped the side of the bus as it pulled away. 'Local island tradition,' he explained.

We were left standing on the side of a deserted road. The dust settled. Just across from us was a small clump of mangroves and a long narrow beach. The day was cloudless.

'Three trips, by my reckoning,' mused Kingy, looking at the supplies and me.

And three trips it was in his small rowing boat. Kingy's red scarf was wringing wet by the time we had completed all three trips.

Then came the slow haul to his cabin on the other side of his island. We did it in one staggered go, with a number of rests on the way.

Then I saw it. My new place of work for the next few weeks.

I settled in very quickly. The place was primitive in many ways, but Kingy was efficient and well organised.

On the domestic front I learned to hand-pump water from a deep well that Kingy had dug just back from the beach, which provided drinking water and cold showers. I learned to start the generator when there was insufficient sunlight to make solar power for his limited power requirements.

I showed him a thing or two he could do with his old Mac that he hadn't been able to sort out. He showed me how to use his Mac when linked to satellite communications systems. He wasn't completely isolated—he had basic email—but there were very strict restrictions on any activity that consumed unnecessary power.

It was his lab that really got my attention. It was full of rats in cages—different sizes, different colours, some with small litters, others working out how to spring traps to release small quantities of food and a number just resting and watching. Some were quite large.

'Not thinking of getting a flute?' joked Kingy, from the adjacent room.

'Actually, it was a pipe,' I corrected with mock superiority. 'Only if you get me a yellow and red cloak,' I replied.

'I'll speak to the town mayor,' Kingy called.

Very seriously I said, 'I think I smell a rat!'

I was actually surprised at how little smell there was. There may not have been much of an odour, but there was a lot of excited noise!

It suddenly occurred to me that the rats weren't just watching me, they were observing and assessing my presence.

Kingy interrupted my thoughts. 'Plenty of rats and not a rat trap to be found!' I silently took in the scene.

I quickly learned the ropes of his small establishment.

On one occasion we tested the rats in a complicated maze. Kingy had made it himself. The beauty of it was that it could be put together like a child's play toy. Parts were removable and adjustable to such an extent that by using the same basic framework Kingy could construct a variety of different mazes. It was covered with bird wire he had salvaged from some flotsam found on his beach. 'Appropriate technology,' he called it with a wry smile.

On this particular day we were testing various rats through the maze. The rats were all known by coded titles. Kingy would make predictions about how long a particular rat would take to solve the maze puzzle.

'Rat 01D2—Hamblin. He'll be slow, I'd wager. Not a leader in the rat world. More the following type,' he grinned.

I noted times and some of Kingy's comments on each rat's attempt to get through the maze.

His cat wandered into the lab. 'Macavity, well now, not looking for a quick feed, I hope. Or are you here to see Eddy?'

We had met on the day I arrived. Macavity, the old ginger cat, was a regular visitor to the lab. He was at home among the rats and shelves and bottles. Kingy said he would sit on the microscope bench for hours and just watch him work—a silent and caring companion.

We continued recording data.

'This one I call Einstein. D0137 for the records. Young Einstein here will do it all in less than a minute. He seems to have a photographic memory. Even when I change the orientation of the whole maze, he seems to be able to take that into account.'

I didn't jot down the comment about a rat with a photographic memory.

Einstein finished, as predicted, in record time. He was rewarded with a titbit of food.

'Just to prove a point, I'll let you create a new maze and we'll see how he goes,' Kingy said.

I made what I thought was a pretty good maze. No patterns in the number of right or left turns. No predictability in the number of openings or dead ends.

'I'll wager a week's salary I can slow him down,' I boasted jovially. 'After all, I've been to uni!'

'For one half of one semester! Sounds like a little knowledge can be a dangerous thing!' he laughed.

I gave an evil smirk as I put a thick book under one end of the maze to give it a tilt. To top it off I threw an old towel across most of the bird wire.

Kingy pursed his lips in a pretend 'that's-not-fair' way.

He placed Einstein in the maze with a tight-lipped grin that said, 'Let's see who's the smart one now.'

The increased darkness of the maze and the disorientation of the sloping floor was not really a complicating factor for Einstein. He completed the maze in record time.

Kingy looked from under his eyebrows as he took Einstein from the framework. From the cradle of his arm Einstein seemed to give me a supercilious look.

Macavity—hissed softly from his bench vantage point.

He's jealous, I thought, but the look on his face was more like contempt.

I shrugged. I wasn't going to worry about it. Nothing gets better than this I mused blithely.

Chapter 5

I soon got to know most of the rats individually. They all had their own personalities and idiosyncrasies. They all had penetrating, watching eyes. Eyes that watched and waited.

One day, when I was in a flippant mood, I glared back at them, my head thrust forward. 'See if you can out-stare me, Mr Beady-eyes!' I challenged the rats in general.

Most of them turned away at this blatant confrontation, but I could see their eyes smouldering when they looked back at me. I could feel their contempt! Did they want to make me to feel like an intruder? I wondered. A threat?

It was one evening later, while I was looking over Kingy's shoulder watching him enter some data into a table on the computer, that I had a strange feeling. I shuddered. I turned around and noticed one rat watching us with particular interest. The only light in the room came from the computer screen. He stared straight at me, almost belligerently. The stare turned to a smirk—I swear it. I felt the hairs on the back of my neck prickle.

It was Einstein. Other eyes glowed a soft green in the dimness of the cages further towards the back of the lab.

Kingy sensed my distraction.

He turned and was quiet for a few moments. 'Ah, Einstein. Trying to see your results. Confidential, you know!'

By this stage Einstein had turned away and was innocently sniffing along the edges of his cage.

'I think he was watching us!' I said.

'Not much else to do if you're locked up in a cage all day just waiting to be fed. Rats really do have a bad reputation. They are always associated with death and decay. And plagues.'

Rightly so, I thought. Take the Great Plague in London, for example! 'The Black Death!' I offered, more confident than I should have been.

'Caused by the bite of an infected rat flea,' Kingy replied.

That clears that up, I thought, amused by my own lack of general knowledge.

Kingy continued, 'They're also associated with leaving sinking ships. A sign of disaster. On the other hand rats going onto a new ship is a good sign. No one tells you that! Rats contain the souls of old men and should be respected. Just think, I could come back as a rat and get the respect I deserve!'

I raised my eyes to the ceiling—well, the underside of the roof. Kingy laughed at himself.

'Of course, if the rat enters a person's house and starts chewing furniture then someone is about to die! There's some ratty trivia for you!'

'Doesn't give us much of a chance. We're loaded with rats in this house!' I joked.

'Maybe it's not all bad,' he continued. 'The Hindus believe that the rat is a symbol of a successful endeavour. It represents prudence and foresight. That's more my style.'

He may have wished he had had a little of that foresight as events unfolded.

Later that night I came in from outside, where I had been watching the nightly migration of fruit bats on the forage, and walked into the lab as Kingy was about to feed the rats. He was crouched down at a small gas fridge getting food for his rats—a mixture of vitamin pills and selected chemical and hormone concoctions mixed up in a little more traditional rat food.

There was nothing sinister in what Kingy was doing. He was innocently going about his chores, oblivious of my presence, when Macavity walked in. I'd seen him in there before, on numerous occasions. To him the rats were part of the furniture.

This time, as he entered between my legs to see what Kingy was up to, he hesitated, looked up at the rat cages and arched his back momentarily. I looked to see what had caused the reaction.

It was Einstein. He was standing in a defiant pose, up on his hind legs. A number of other rats were watching intently.

The moment he saw me he dropped to all fours and turned away, but I was sure he was still watching me out of the corner of his eye. He was acting like someone who had just committed a fiendish deed.

I was about to say something when Kingy spoke. 'Ah, Macavity, the rats' friend. Well, at least, not their mortal foe. Where have you been all day?'

Macavity gave another look towards the caged rodents and left, tail in the air.

'What would cats know about the finer points of rats anyway?' Kingy called to his departed presence.

The incident in itself was so small that I soon forgot about it until it resurfaced much later.

Chapter 6

My stay with Kingy finally came to an end. It had been good even if, towards the end, Kingy became more and more absorbed in his work and let me carry on the routine stuff almost without interruption.

We spent many fine tropical evenings sitting on the steps that faced the open sea discussing theories of evolution and the feasibility of accelerated change. We talked about modifying animal behaviour by rewards and punishment. We became good colleagues.

Macavity would nestle under Kingy's bent knees and then Kingy would gently stroke his back or tickle him under the chin.

'You'd be lost without that cat,' I said, breaking the silence one balmy evening.

'Hate to admit it,' he nodded, 'but the cat's a better companion than any rat!'

'Macavity, Macavity, there's no one like Macavity,' I began reciting.

Then Kingy chimed in. 'For he's a fiend in feline shape, a monster of depravity.'

We laughed together. 'A student with a knowledge of poetry! What's the world coming to?' Kingy chuckled.

Looking at Macavity at that moment I could not imagine the old ginger cat getting involved in any depraved acts.

'Hey,' said Kingy, 'how about some cat trivia?'

'Cats bring good luck—or is it bad? I've never been sure.'

'Depends where you come from,' Kingy reflected.

I thought for another moment, then said, 'Cats have nine lives!'

Kingy gave a soft snort. 'Hardly trivia!' He was quiet for a moment and stroked Macavity's upright tail. 'You know, it would suit me fine if Macavity had a few more lives. I'll miss the old fella when he goes. In cat years I'm sure he must be over sixty'

That's how it was on many evenings. Kingy and I and Macavity, sharing companionship, ideas, personal thoughts and trivia.

They were good times, but my visit had to come to an end. For my own safety I had to return home. I'm sure my father would have drafted me off to a labour camp at a Siberian salt mine if I hadn't returned in time for my uni lectures.

I had had such a rewarding time and Kingy was so glad to have had the professional company that we agreed to do it all again when I got my next break from uni. Reluctantly I had to admit that I had developed a new-found enthusiasm for my studies. There was no way I was going to be a swot, but I was going to do some work when I got back to uni!

To make things more convenient, Kingy had even fixed up a small boat for me out of the hull of one he'd found decaying under his verandah.

As I rowed across the shallows I actually felt some regrets. I was pleased that the wait for the bus was short and left no time for me to get morbid. I allowed myself one last glance at the place that had become my second home as the bus crossed the little bridge, and then I focused on the realities of my return to civilisation.

I did save a forlorn wave for the leaning signpost on the track to Buka Buka Village, reflecting for one brief moment on Kingy's unexpected gruffness when we first passed that spot.

Chapter 7

Several weeks after arriving home I received an email from Kingy. I was quite excited when I saw his name flash in the New Mail list.

To: EddyHaite@iserve.com
From: king@iserve.com
Subject: Touching base—update

Hi Eddy, from the isle of swaying palms

(Did you know rats can actually climb palm trees? They eat the immature fruit. Another bit of ratty trivia.)

I have been very busy. Getting some really way-out results regarding intelligence modification.

I'm sure my figures are right but will check them again. If there is still a problem we'll both have a look at them when next you visit. 00B7 (Einstein) is showing quite remarkable achievement. A number of others are heading down this strange track. I've redesigned the maze to take a small team of rats at the same time. There always seems to be a leader emerge that guides the less intelligent (??) members through. Guess who is emerging as a strong leader?

I let Einstein out of his cage every so often. He doesn't run away. Actually, the truth is, I have found him out of his cage on occasions. I must be getting forgetful and not pushing the bolt right across. He'd soon notice that! It's not a problem. The island is really a huge cage (prison??), they are extremely unlikely to escape to the mainland and create environ-mental havoc.

Out of the cage he just wanders around inspecting the other cages. Sometimes I think he talks to them. (I've been living alone too long!) I talk to them too—and the cat! Sometimes he sits on my shoulder as I type. The screen seems to fascinate him.

A few of the rats are showing signs of a malaise—maybe the chemicals are having side effects. I wonder about the effects of radiation in umpteen generations of rats. Some have stopped eating and one has died. Lost the will to live. Couldn't find any obvious reason for its death. A few of the other seem very listless. We could talk about it when you come—I'm open to a bit of original thought right now. Been feeling that way myself a

bit lately. Dull headaches, tired eyes.
Overwork? Stress of modern living!!

Kingy

(King of Wolfe Island!)

Maybe Kingy had a dietary problem. How much sweet potato and dry biscuit can one man eat?

I spoke to Holly Turner, a girl I had met on campus, about dietary problems. She was into health foods in a big way. She admitted not knowing much about tropical foods. She was a little sceptical about a scientist living on a tropical island and doing experiments with rats.

I thought a bit about the problem rats but I couldn't come up with a rational explanation without more information.

There was the possibility of a genetic throwback, but I was sure Kingy would have thought of that and tested the theory. He was very methodical.

It was good to hear from him at any rate, and good to hear that he was making progress.

I sent a short reply soon after receiving his email. There was nothing urgent in it—it might be days before he logged onto his email.

I put Kingy at the back of my mind and concentrated as much on my social activities as I did on my studies.

Kingy's next email was a little more perplexing.

To: EddyHaite@iserve.com
From: king@iserve.com
Subject: update

Eddy,

I think I'm losing track of all my research. My headaches are getting worse. Have no idea what is causing them. Can't concentrate too long on intense work.

Still losing some of my rats. Some of the nicer, quieter ones. No idea what's the cause! 00B7 (Einstein) is becoming quite a rat. He definitely has some sort of charisma. He seems to be finding ways out of his cage I'm sure. I keep a checklist of bolting the cage each night. Sounds like I'm going senile. I'm not.

Then maybe I am. I have misplaced some of my important notes and I'll have to redo some of the experiments again.

Looking forward to your return. I could use more than a lab assistant at times. Hell of an ache in the back of my head. Bring a whole batch of super strong painkillers when you come—would be appreciated. Kingy

(King of Wolfe Island!)

I sat in front of my computer, swinging gently on the back legs of my chair for a few minutes, reflecting on what I had read. There was more amiss than Kingy realised, or was letting on.

I opened the earlier email and re-read it.

Two thoughts struck me. The second email was shorter and less positive than the first.

The first email bubbled with enthusiasm. The new one was almost a plea for help not at all like the Kingy I knew.

I fired back a quick businesslike reply. I said I was sorry about the lost reports and his headaches. I made no comment about the rats. I mentioned possible arrival dates saying it all depended on the local transport at his end.

I hoped for a quick response. It took over a week.

> To: EddyHaite@iserve.com
>
> From: king@iserve.com
>
> Subject: good news
>
> Eddy,
>
> So pleasedd to here you are coming. Looking forw2ard too getting back on track again. i bring you up to date when you get here. Had some generator trouble the last few day. Some of the wires had frayed throught and I took a while to sort it.

```
I'll get this of before anything else
goes wrong. Don't foprget the headache
pills and could you get me some new
floppy disks. Something else I seemed to
have lost Kingy

(King of Wolfe Island!)
```

The spelling was atrocious. The email had not been proofed very well. It wasn't at all like the critical Kingy I had come to know.

It sounded like he was experiencing some stressful times. It was not what I expected from someone who had been a self-sufficient loner for most of his adult life.

I finalised my plans to return to Wolfe Island. I had a nagging feeling it was going to be very different from my first visit.

Chapter 8

As the bus rattled across the wooden bridge, Wolfe Island came into view. No doubt it was just as pretty as ever, but I was seeing it with different eyes. It looked isolated and solitary. On the horizon there were heavy storm clouds rising high into the stratosphere. It wasn't an unusual sight for the tropics, but today they seemed particularly ominous.

After leaving the bus and giving it the ritual thump on the side, I lugged my two cram-packed bags to the shore—a suitcase and a sports bag. My backpack weighed heavily on my shoulders. I also had a plastic bag of goodies I had picked up in town.

My boat was still where I had left it. Some vines had grown over the bow and a small pool of brackish water lay on the floor, which was covered with decaying leaves. It hadn't been touched since I last left.

I tipped the boat onto its side, disturbing some hermit crabs in the process. The water drained out, leaving a thin coating of black sludge. The single seat was dry and clean.

I placed my bags in as carefully as possible, hoping the muck would clean off without too much sweat. I rowed across to the island as the tide was going out, being careful not to run into the outcrops of coral that lay just below the surface. The water in the channel ran strongly and I had to put in a concerted effort to prevent the little boat from being rushed off course.

When I relaxed and looked up I was surprised to see a small bamboo raft heading away from the western edge of the island. Two men carrying what looked like primitive barge poles were standing on the raft. Though they were some distance away they seemed to be watching me cross the channel to the island.

Local fishermen, I thought, without being too concerned.

On the little beach I removed my bags and dragged the boat above the high water line, next to Kingy's boat.

I had just entered the track to the cabin, struggling under the weight and awkward-ness of my luggage, when I saw a movement just to the right of the track. I paused and Macavity came out of the tangle of scrub. He looked at me suspiciously.

As I lowered my bags I said, 'Hey Mac, it's me.'

He didn't come forward, so I took a few non-threatening steps in his direction. 'Hey, hey. That's not much of a welcome.'

Even from a distance he looked bedraggled. His ginger fur looked unkempt. I'd seen alley cats in a similar condition. I put it down to his wandering around in the tangle of vegetation.

He was tense, ready to run, so I stopped and spoke softly to him. 'Hey, you been losing a bit of weight. Not getting fed?

Bet it's too much sweet potato and coconut and not enough fish, eh? Or is it the rats?'

I squatted down, hoping I would be a less formidable sight. The sudden movement made him flee to the safety of the undergrowth.

I pouted in the direction he had vanished and collected my bags for the final burst of energy to the cabin.

Even as I entered the clearing around the cabin I could tell that things were not quite right—that things weren't as ordered as they normally were. Kingy was normally someone who had 'a place for everything and everything in its place'.

There was a bit of litter near the back door and some broken branches lying scattered in the cleared area. Obviously they had fallen off the giant rain trees that surrounded the site. A few dead palm fronds had been dragged carelessly to one side. It was nothing spectacular, but it wasn't at all like Kingy.

He suddenly emerged through the back door, wearing his bright red scarf. I'm sure he hadn't taken it off since I had left. He hadn't known exactly when to expect me, but when he saw me he was all smiles. He almost loped across the space to hug me. I only just managed to get my bags onto the ground.

He was full of questions and kept saying how glad he was to see me. He tried to take both bags as well as usher me forward.

'Kingy,' I said in exasperation, 'slow down.'

He laughed, almost dropped the bags and bear-hugged me again.

We celebrated my return with my goodies: warm Coke and half a packet of less-than-crisp chocolate chip biscuits I had managed to pick up in town.

Kingy was delighted with the surprise. We talked about things in general and I rummaged in one of my bags for the items he had asked for. He nodded his approval of the floppy disks and read the label of the painkillers thoroughly.

'Should be good stuff! Get me back on track, I hope,' he murmured.

'Had some visitors?' I remarked, suddenly remembering the men on the raft.

Kingy looked at me quizzically then shook his head.

I didn't pursue the matter. It didn't seem important.

Slowly he began to talk about his problems. He wasn't sure if he was getting forgetful and careless or if it was something more alarming.

'Almost lost the microscope one night. Must have left it right on the edge of the bench and it got knocked off,' he said.

'Knocked off? Stolen?' I said with alarm.

'No, no. Not that "knocked off". Macavity, I guess. Sure wasn't a burglar!' he laughed. 'Still, he isn't that sort of careless cat—or wasn't. Odd.'

I told him about seeing Macavity up along the track.

'That's unusual for him, too—well, it was once. He used to be a real house cat. Odd again!'

'Then there was the problem with the genny. No power for a few wet days. Couldn't use the computer. Maybe it's all getting too much for me.'

'Need a holiday?'

'Yeah, some nice isolated tropical paradise—with nothing to worry about and nobody to distract me.' He was quiet for a while and we watched the sun sink behind the storm clouds on the horizon. By now they were little more than a distant feature of the scene.

'Had a few problems with some of the rats. Some terrible behaviour patterns were developing. Totally unpredictable. Real aggressive. Real mean aggressiveness. And usually without cause. I keep a strict record of their diet. They all have the same concoction unless I'm looking into variables. Upset me, it did.'

I looked at him for an explanation.

'Eventually had to put them down. You should have heard the din when I took them from their cages. It was as if I had gone in there with a butcher's knife. They seemed to know my inner motives.'

'Einstein as well?'

'No, strangely. I get the impression he's capable of a lot of things, but no. He just watched. Taking it all in.' He paused. 'I'm getting fanciful, I fear.'

Macavity appeared out of the bush. He came forward like a combat soldier, watching every which way

'Speak of the devil!' I said suddenly.

We looked at each other and shrugged, then shook our heads.

By this time the first fruit bats were lumbering across the sky on their evening quest for mature fruit.

'Must be feed time. For Macavity, as well as the crew in the lab. Come on Macca, old fellow, let's go.' Kingy got up and went inside. I followed like the dutiful assistant I was.

Macavity was still a bit wary, but he was getting used to my presence.

We went into the lab. I looked around. It was much the same as when I had left, but there was a feeling that things were fraying at the edges, and there was a distinct, but faint, ratty smell. The familiar sound of ratty excitement was present too.

This time I refrained from saying, 'I smell a rat.' It seemed somehow inappropriate.

When I walked in behind Kingy the noise almost stopped for a moment before starting up again, as if I was some unexpected visitor—which I suppose I was.

I glanced around the room at the rats. Most of them were getting excited about being fed. A few were watching Kingy open the little fridge and prepare the food. I noticed that Einstein was watching me intently. It made me uneasy for some reason. He turned away as if bored by my presence, and I had a strange feeling that it was all a sham, an act.

Involuntarily I thought, What a ham! I was surprised by the thought.

I turned and saw Macavity lurking back from the doorway. I called him softly. He hissed quietly and came no closer.

'Won't come in here any more. Can't drag him in. Rip my arms off if I tried!'

'That's a bit of a change,' I offered. 'Might be scared of doing some more damage.'

'It looks to me as if he's acquired an aversion to rats. I guess it's possible, but not very probable.'

'Is there a word for a phobia about rats?' I asked in jest.

'That's a good one. I don't know,' Kingy admitted with a satisfied smile. I had stumped him on rat trivia!

It was then he asked me to check all the bolts on the cages. 'I'm sure they're all in place.'

They were. All the bolts had been slid through as far as they would go and the little handle knobs were turned into their securing slots.

That night as I lay on my sleeping bag I thought about the rats. There had been a subtle change in their overall behaviour, but I couldn't quite place what it was.

As night deepened the sound of the sea intensified. The crashing waves on the outer reef, which I hardly noticed during the day, now had a muted roar like traffic on a distant highway.

I drifted off into a shallow sleep with visions of being watched by Einstein and the sounds of fruit bats noisily fighting over wild pawpaw in the nearby jungle.

Chapter 9

The next morning I made my way into the lab. Kingy was already there, tapping on the keys of his Mac. He had a found a new burst of energy. He gave me a quick smile and a quick thumbs up and returned his attention to his monitor.

There was an air of purpose about the place, even though not much had physically changed. Even the rats seemed a little less scatty.

I set about straightening things up, clearing away bits of rubbish. I became completely absorbed in my menial tasks, but I felt relaxed anyway.

It was when I turned to straightening up the cages that I noticed one of the cages had its bolt handle in the unsecured position. The cage belonged to one of the more active rats. It watched me as I examined my oversight of the previous night.

I was sure I had checked them all and fastened them securely, but I can be prone to making mistakes sometimes. I often misplace lecture notes and I have a long history of forgetting the 'date due' for assignments.

On impulse I checked all the cages. I found seven that had their bolts unsecured. That was too many for carelessness, even on my part.

One of the cages was Einstein's.

As I pushed the bolt into position he watched me from the far corner of his cage. I looked up just in time to notice a number of the other rats staring at me.

I told Kingy of my neglect, careful not to make too much of it and be seen as an incompetent assistant.

'Probably an oversight. Not a problem,' he said as he tapped away at his keys. As far as he was concerned no damage had been done.

I wondered for a moment, then gave a shrug.

Later that morning Kingy told me a little more about his problems with his rats. Some of them had refused to participate in the maze experiments.

'At first I put it down to a possible dietary problem, maybe fatigue—couldn't believe that though! Maybe the heat, the humidity. Then I thought about some developmental abnormality. Had to reject all those grand theories because the rats behaved normally when put back in their cages.'

I was tempted to ask what he considered was normal for these rats, but instead I pompously suggested, 'Maybe it's the long term effects of residual radiation. Gamma rays? X rays? Beta rays?'

Kingy looked at me askance, as if too much knowledge, in my case, was a dangerous thing. Laconically he said, 'What about stingrays and manta rays? Plenty of those around the island.'

He was silent for a moment, before speaking again. 'No, they're simply refusing to cooperate!' he admitted with mock indignation. 'They're like defiant children!'

It took a moment for me to realise that defiance could be a good thing. The rats might have been getting bored, which might have been a sign of increased intelligence. All Kingy had to do was find a way to monitor it.

Casually I asked, 'Any rats in particular?'

He thought about it for a moment then pointed to several of the cages. 'Yes, generally those ones.' Then he added, as if pondering the point, 'Mostly males.'

I was momentarily shocked, though I tried not to show it. The rats he had indicated were the same rats that had had their bolts tampered with.

That night I insisted that Kingy and I check the bolts together so that there could be no mistakes. He must have thought it was a waste of time, but he humoured me nevertheless.

The rats were quieter than usual—a little less restless, but in the dimming lights of the weakening backup batteries, I felt our actions were being followed by alert eyes.

I was the restless one. It took a while for me to get to sleep and when I did it wasn't a deep sleep. I put it down to the percussion of the night insects that disturbed the silent stillness of the jungle. I don't like coincidences. There's something unscientific about coincidences.

I was up just as dawn broke. The early morning chorus of birds had just begun. The southern sky was a pink, pearly hue.

I decided on a short beach walk before facing the 'unexpected' in the lab. I went barefoot onto the tide-washed sand. It was still cool and damp.

It was a bit of a shock to discover another set of footprints. I was sure Kingy hadn't left the house. The thought that they could have been Kingy's was quickly discarded. The prints were too big.

I looked up and down the beach, not sure what I was expecting to see. I tried peering into the early morning shadows of the beach vegetation. Nothing.

I felt a bit like Robinson Crusoe the day he found the footprints of Friday on his beach. I followed the prints along the beach.

Every so often they would disappear where the wash of a larger wave had swept up onto the beach.

To my surprise, or maybe dismay, I suddenly came upon a second set of prints. There was not just one man but two men. Momentarily I questioned why I had assumed they were the prints of men. It was more to do with the size rather than any real evidence.

I stopped and sucked at my lips. Evidently the second person had been walking in the shallow water of the small waves as they ran up the beach.

Where are they now? I thought with growing alarm. What were they doing on the island anyway?

Then my imagination kicked in like an angry mule. Why had I assumed that there were only two? There could have been a third person walking in the water. Or a fourth! Or a fifth!

Was there a whole a group of natives out there waiting to attack me, then take over the house?

I thought about the security in the house and the lab. There was none!

I kept walking down the beach, away from the house, following the footsteps but irrationally not treading on them in case I was destroying some sort of evidence.

I was near the end of the beach when I looked up at a little outcrop of ancient coral rock. Sitting in the meagre shade of a pandanus tree, half hidden by small coastal brush, were two men. Their bodies were dark against the early morning sky.

I guessed they had been watching me from the time I'd left the house. No doubt they had followed my progress down the beach. For a moment my feelings were a confused mixture of foolishness and misgivings.

Then they stood up and I could see they were wearing shorts and T-shirts, but no shoes. They considered my presence for a moment and, with what looked like a casual wave, picked up their bundles of gear and headed off along the rocky point before disappearing.

Suddenly I was alone again. Then, when I looked back along the beach, the incoming waves had washed away most of the footprints. The whole incident might not have happened at all.

I turned back to the coral outcrop in time to see a bamboo raft emerge from behind a distant overhang of coastal trees. It was making its way west, out near the reef but still inside the lagoon.

A pair of agitated terns whirled and dived above the sparkling sea.

I shrugged. It was time to go back.

Chapter 10

First thing next morning I went straight to the lab and began inspecting the doors of the cages. All the bolts were in place except two belonging to Einstein and a rat I'd nicknamed Rastus.

Impatiently I pushed the bolts into the secure position, more than a little worried. It was then that I noticed the small fridge door was slightly ajar. There were too many unexplained things happening.

I pushed the door shut firmly and glanced back towards the rats. None of them were looking at me. They were all preoccupied with other activities.

Kingy was just coming out of the shower. He had nothing on except a lap-lap. His red scarf hung over his shoulder. I told him of my discoveries about the rats.

He threw his hands up in the air in a display of complete exasperation. 'Just what are you trying to tell me?' he yelled. 'Can't I have a moment's peace before breakfast before you come running to me with silly little discoveries?'

I backed off with a series of 'sorries' and went for a hurried walk down to the beach to recover my composure. Indignantly I told myself I had done nothing wrong.

I glared at the beach, searching for foot-prints, but it was high tide.

There was a coconut lying in the sand the size of a deformed junior soccer ball. I began dribbling it along the soft sand, weaving in and out of the pieces of dead coral.

At the end of the beach I turned. I wanted to give the coconut one good angry kick. Something made me look up guiltily. Kingy was standing there with a mug of steaming black tea in each hand. 'I'm sorry,' he said simply. 'I don't know what came over me.' He shrugged and handed me the tea. 'Peace offering?'

'Accepted.'

We walked in silence for a few minutes before he spoke again. 'Had one of my headaches last night. Not real bad, but a headache! Not much sleep. I had no reason to take it out on you.'

We turned and walked back towards the cabin. The waves roared on the outer reef. My anger subsided like the sea after a tropical squall.

He continued. 'Have you noticed that even the rats are less of a problem since your return? Well, I don't actually know if you could, you weren't here before your return … but you seem to have a calming influence on the place. Me included.'

As I worked I pondered over Kingy's words. It was just a little odd that in a couple of days I could have brought calm to the lab! To me it seemed more like the rats were biding time, waiting for some opportunity to present itself. In a more rational moment I might have found that idea a bit far-fetched.

The good news was that, for the moment, it felt as if things were getting back onto an even keel. Even Macavity ventured closer to the door. He would wander right up to it, have an inquisitive look, then back off. We hadn't made that much progress.

Later I had misgivings over not telling Kingy about the two visitors I'd seen on the beach. I was more than a little worried that it might upset him. I also knew it might upset him more if he found out I hadn't told him. I'm caught between a rock and a coral reef, I thought wryly to myself.

An opportunity arose during our morning tea break. We were sitting on the steps overlooking the beach.

'Had some early morning visitors,' I said as casually as I could, then waited for an outburst.

Kingy looked at me inquiringly. I told him about my experience on the beach, and how I'd felt like Robinson Crusoe.

He was quiet for a moment. He didn't seem all that thrilled about the visitors. Then he said, 'Probably from Buka Buka. They actually have traditional fishing rights along this section of coast and around the island. Trouble is, they still think they have hunting and gathering rights on the island. The rights lapsed ages ago and they were compensated fully by the government.'

'Hunting?' I said. 'What? Fruit bats?'

'It wouldn't be surprising, but they're probably more interested in the land crabs and bread-tree fruit,' Kingy mused with a bit of a sneer.

He was silent for a moment. 'I think the hunting and fishing is more of an excuse to get onto the island. I think they're a suspicious bunch. Probably afraid of my work or my presence here. Anything that seems covert makes some of them suspicious, like they're being left out or cheated. I bet they wouldn't mind seeing what's going on behind these walls. I guess that can lead to some illogical resentment.'

'Do they know what you're doing?'

'No way! They can't see any reason for our being here. They probably resent that a bit too. They don't like to be kept in the dark.'

'We might have some rats like that,' I suggested lightly.

Kingy laughed softly as he threw the last of his tea onto the sand.

For a while after that we seemed to be getting back on track.

Chapter 11

Kingy's next outburst caught me by surprise. I heard a sudden string of angry swearing from the lab. The rats started squealing frantically.

As I reached the door I could see Kingy standing in front of his Mac, only just managing to restrain himself from putting his fist through it. He turned angrily, kicking his wooden chair out of the way.

He then swore with such anger that I almost stepped back from the office door.

He saw me. 'What the hell are you looking at?' he shouted.

I was struck dumb. I had no idea what had gone wrong.

'Well?' he demanded.

His eyes were bloodshot and blazing. His thinning hair was hanging down in ragged strands.

'Just came to see if I could help.' I was shaking inside. I had never seen such anger in a grown man before.

'You can help by leaving me alone!' He pulled at the red scarf he had knotted around his neck. I could see that his teeth were clenched.

I turned to leave, muttering a mildly sarcastic comment.

Behind me I heard a thump. I turned around. Kingy had crumpled into a heap onto the lab floor. I rushed to his aid, dragging him to the next room.

The rats had suddenly turned very quiet.

I managed to get Kingy into the most comfortable chair in the kitchen. He folded his arms on the table and rested his head there. For a moment I thought he was about to start sobbing. I didn't know what to do. I hadn't had any experience with adults crying.

'Could you make a cup of tea, please?' he said, without looking up.

I muttered a few words about needing time to relax and settle down and then went to make the tea.

He said no more until I put the tea before him. Slowly, ever so slowly, he raised his head. His eyes were puffy. 'Another apology. Sorry, sorry, sorry.'

All I could say was, 'It's OK. Want to tell me about it?'

He sat silently for a while, just sipping his tea. When he was ready he explained how he had had a restless night and a headache that seemed to get worse the longer he lay in bed.

'Might be a migraine?' I suggested. I knew migraines could be bad. Mum gets them occasionally. 'Can I get you a couple of painkillers?'

He shook his head and continued to tell me how he had been transferring data from one folder to another when a rat had run across his keyboard. He had been so shocked that he had accidentally deleted some valuable material. Worse still, he had accidentally disconnected his Mac from the power supply while trying to get the rat, losing all the work that he hadn't saved. He hadn't been thinking clearly at all.

'Maybe I should upgrade the old Mac,' he said wistfully. 'Get one from Government Supplies!' Then laughed, without mirth.

Tentatively, to keep him talking, I suggested that maybe it was time to end the experiments before something drastic happened.

He was tempted to agree with me, but he was not about to give up his life's work.

I told him to take his time with his tea and that I'd do what I could in the lab. I didn't like the idea of rats running free.

I couldn't find the rat and I checked all the cages. No rat appeared to be missing. The rats watched me as I made my inspection. Something was definitely wrong. This latest outburst was more than a bit of a worry. I plugged in the Mac. It came on very slowly. I thought for a moment it was about to freeze, but it finally came back to life.

There was another outburst a day or so later. It followed much the same course as the previous one. This time Kingy was having trouble with the water pump. The priming mechanism had become clogged with some foreign matter, which turned out to be bits of plastic biscuit wrapper.

His outburst was out of proportion to the problem. I thought it might all be getting too much for him.

'Back off a bit,' I urged under my breath. 'It ain't worth it!'

To make things worse there was an unexplained deterioration in some of his better rat specimens. They weren't ill, but something was making them become more than just scatty. They became nasty and unco-operative and were extremely wary of the food they ate. If they had been people, I thought wryly, I would have put it down to some form of anorexia!

I wasn't game to joke about it for fear of another outburst.

Kingy didn't like killing them.

One day after the most recent cull, as we sat in the lab on a couple of stools, I tentatively but seriously suggested aborting the experiments.

I waited for his reaction.

Slowly he said, 'I have considered the idea in the dead of night. In fact I've given it some serious thought. But in the light of day I guess I'm a little more rational.' He gave a funny little laugh. 'I am sure that once I'm over whatever's ailing me, I'll be OK.'

I wondered, but I said nothing.

Chapter 12

This was followed by another strange and worrying event.

One day while standing outside the lab I peered in through the grimy window. I could see Rastus in his cage. I had been attracted to the glass by the film of accumulated dried salt. Absent-mindedly I rubbed it with my finger, leaving a line of clear glass.

Rastus's cage was near the window. He was standing on his hind haunches as if he was a lookout.

I cleared a little more of the glass, careful not to attract his attention. It was then that I saw Einstein—out of his cage and running across the top of some of the other cages, dropping what looked like bits of food into a number of them. I could hardly believe my eyes. As I watched, Rastus suddenly let out a squeal. Einstein immediately changed course and headed for his own cage, pulling the door closed with his tail.

Kingy came in and gave the lab a casual once-over glance and then switched on his computer. His eyes looked tired and his face drawn.

As I was about to step back I saw Rastus turn his head towards the window. I could almost feel the hate in his eyes.

I hurried around to the lab door. I started to speak, 'Kingy …'

But when I looked in, the place was peaceful.

Kingy grunted a welcome without looking up.

I slipped past Kingy to Einstein's cage. The bolt was more or less in place but the handle was not in the securing slot. I was about to tell Kingy, but I hesitated and the moment passed.

Rastus looked up from a sleeping position and studied my reaction. I suddenly realised how big he had grown. I felt cold and clammy and made a quick exit to the sunny beach, where I could collect my wild thoughts.

'Need a walk,' I casually informed Kingy as I left the lab.

If he replied I didn't hear him.

Later, Kingy had another minor outburst. This time it was about misplacing his painkillers. I found them on the floor of the lab, under the computer desk.

'How the hell did they get there?' he said in an exasperated voice as I handed him the soiled pack.

I had no answer, but I was starting to develop all sorts of wild theories. I kept them to myself, but again I pressed Kingy about aborting or at least modifying the experiments. He was unconvinced. I'm not very persuasive at times. Persuasive argument is not one of my strong points. I'm not a debating team kind of guy.

Both times that I had spoken about aborting the program we had been in the lab, which wasn't unusual since we spent most of our time in there, but I remember now how peaceful the lab had been on those two occasions. I sometimes had this wild idea that the rats had been listening to us, considering their options.

If that wasn't suspicious enough, on a few occasions I had noticed Kingy half rise from his computer and quickly glance out the window. Once or twice I had seen him lift his head from his workbench and look to the beach or the ocean. The first time I saw him do it I thought he might have seen something unusual. Not wanting to miss out on something interesting, I joined him at the window.

'What is it?' I asked innocently. I couldn't see anything out of the ordinary as I surveyed the beach and the sea. The sky was empty too.

He seemed embarrassed, like a child who had been caught doing something inappropriate. 'Just watching the sea,' he offered vaguely as he returned his attention to his work. But his mind seemed preoccupied with other thoughts.

I was becoming concerned for Kingy. It wasn't anything definite, but there were little pointers. If only I could work out where they were pointing.

There were the problems with the rats: their cages, their eating disorders, their strange behaviour. It could have been part of the ongoing experiment, but I had a feeling that things were fraying at the edges.

Picking up a scrap of paper I turned it over and drew a box. I put a heading over it: RATS. I made some quick notes about things I could remember about the rats.

1. Some rats seem to dislike me/not trust me/resent me.
2. Einstein trying to see results of experiments (I think).
3. Macavity's growing dislike of the rats/ lab.
4. Aggressive, unpredictable behaviour of rats (when I was away), eating disorders.
5. Cage bolts in unsecured position.
6. Rat involved in loss of computer data.
7. Rastus and Einstein 'delivering' food (?) to other caged rats.

Then there was Kingy's headaches and his pills. I was getting worried that he was either taking too many too often or that there were times he would start to take them, then get distracted and then misplace them. This didn't really explain why the packets were turning up in odd places.

I drew another box and put the heading PILLS above it, but I didn't write anything in it. It was all a bit vague.

I wondered if Kingy's headaches might be a symptom of something more serious. I had no idea what that could be. I tried to remember what I had heard about stress-related illnesses. About the only thing I could think of was that it was common among people working in huge organisations. That hardly described the lab on Wolfe Island.

I mused for a moment or two then drew a box headed with the words MAC THE CAT. I could only come up with three points.

1. Wandering around in the jungle—real scraggy.
2. Fear/dislike of rats in lab.
3. Microscope incident—who did it???

Somewhere in the back of my mind were the villagers from Buka Buka. There was nothing sinister there but they seemed to be another aspect of the Wolfe Island situation.

I drew another box in a space at the bottom of the page and labelled it VILLAGERS. I ran out of ideas after two vague points.

1. Seen boating away from island.
2. Seen at far end of beach (been fishing/ spying?)

A sudden thought struck me. I remembered how Kingy was on edge at times, looking out the window, checking the beach. Was that connected to the Buka Buka villagers? Suddenly the idea didn't seem so good, but I wrote a third point anyway:

3. RK on the look-out?

Then I wrote the word GENERATOR and drew a rough ring around it, but then I had nothing to add.

I looked at my five sets of messy data: Pills, Rats, Mac the Cat, Villagers and Generator. I could see no connections. I studied my observations for a few minutes. They were hardly the stuff on which to base any conclusions.

I tapped the pencil on the bench top a few times, trying to make sense of my points. Nothing came to mind. I picked up the paper and screwed it up before tossing it into an old cardboard carton that acted as a waste paper bin. Now it was serving as the 'too hard' basket!

There had been moments when I thought that someone might be trying to sabotage the whole project. These were wild ideas indeed—out of left field as one of my uni friends would say. Who'd be interested in sabotage anyway?

Chapter 13

Although I had discarded my notes and Kingy and I had started to have a more relaxed time, my subconscious was still troubled. I slept uneasily, waking in the middle of the night more than once. The crazy thing was I could toss and turn in my bunk for hours, but then when the first light crept in from the southeast I would drift off into deep sleep until Kingy woke me with his pottering around the kitchen.

Some time later, after one such uneasy sleep I woke, not to breakfast-type noises or the dawn chorus of tropical birds in the jungle canopy, but to an unusual silence.

I rolled over and saw Kingy looking intently out of one of the glassless windows towards the beach. Some of the windows were nothing more than openings in the wall, with timber shutters hinged at the top. They were kept open with long pieces of wood. In bad weather and especially cyclones, the timber supports were removed and the shutters dropped down and bolted into position. I had never seen the shutters in a closed position.

Kingy thumped the window ledge softly but firmly and left the room without looking in my way. I heard him go down the steps in the direction of the beach. I felt a disturbing uneasiness.

As I rolled myself to a sitting position on the bunk I wondered what had caught his attention. It was far too early to be getting excited, I thought sleepily.

It seemed like the beginning of a perfect day. The sky, what I could see of it, was a hazy blue. An indifferent southeast breeze drifted across the room, keeping the temperature comfortable. The smell of salt added a certain freshness.

As I was getting dressed I heard a loudish 'cluck' in the lab. I'm not real quick in the morning, but it didn't take a genius to work out something had made the sound and it wasn't Kingy. He had gone down to the beach.

I made my way into the lab and casually looked around the room. Everything seemed to be in place. The rats were peaceful captives, though a couple looked decidedly drowsy. I wondered if it was Sunday morning.

Kingy's notes were near his Mac in their usual state of orderly confusion. The corners of the loose top pages were gently stirring in the hint of a breeze that came into the lab.

I rubbed my sleepy eyes and stepped forward, peering at the notes that Kingy had been working on. His writing style didn't encourage easy comprehension. I was about to give up when I noticed what looked like ratty footprints across the top page.

Immediately I was alert. I slowly turned my attention to the cages. Everything looked peaceful. Einstein was asleep in the back corner of his cage. A couple of other rats were watching me disinterestedly, as if there was nothing better to do.

I realised that the prints could have been left at any time. It didn't have to be a recent occurrence. The prints were quite faint. I was jumping to conclusions again.

I stood up and stepped back from the desk. It was then that I stood on one of Kingy's pill packets. As it collapsed under my heel I looked down at it with resignation. It was not turning out to be my morning. I stepped back and picked the packet up, hoping I hadn't squashed too may of the pills. It was a relief to find that it was empty. I crushed it in my hand.

I guessed that the wind had blown it off Kingy's desk. There was a glass near his computer containing what appeared to be the white undissolved residue of a pill—or pills.

It didn't make sense. There was only a small breeze in the lab—enough to blow Kingy's notes around, but certainly not strong enough to lift an empty pill packet off the desk.

Of course Kingy might have dropped it or tossed it on the floor. The conclusion satisfied me for a moment until I remembered that it was a noise that had drawn me to the lab in the first place.

It was all too much thought for the first thing in the morning. I needed some breakfast. A mug of instant coffee and a cool piece of pawpaw from the gas fridge.

I was about to turn and leave when a glint of silver paper in one of the cages caught my eye. I couldn't remember ever using anything silver in the cages. I moved in for a closer look.

It looked like silver foil. I wondered where it could have come from. It couldn't be from a cigarette packet. Neither of us smoked. It certainly wasn't off a chocolate bar! The inside of the UHT milk cartons was foil lined, but there was no way I could imagine it getting into a rat's cage.

I thought for a moment and then looked at what I was holding. Pills came in sleeves of foil seals.

I took the bit of paper from the cage and looked at it. It was definitely from a pill packet.

Shaking my head I slipped the retrieved piece into the packet, crushed the packet and tossed the lot into the rubbish box with more force than necessary. I wondered momentarily if I should rewrite my notes, adding another point to the RATS box.

As I left the lab I gave a final glare at the rats. Einstein watched my actions nonchalantly. Did he feel superior to me? With an annoyed shake of my head I concluded that he probably did!

As I took a heavy coffee mug off a hook on the wall I looked out the kitchen window to the beach. I could see Kingy at the water's edge. The sun was more or less behind him, rising above the sea. As Kingy ran his fingers impatiently through his thinning hair it briefly flared as it caught the early sun.

With him were two locals, dressed in shorts and well-worn T-shirts, the foamy waves washing their bare feet with every sally onto the beach. I guessed they were from Buka Buka Village. One held a stick of some sort, which was stuck into the sand near his feet.

I could see they were having quite a discussion. It wasn't just idle gossip. Kingy started waving his arms around to emphasise a point.

The two local men were certainly unmoved by what he was saying.

Chapter 14

I couldn't hear what the trio was discussing. The smallest of breakers running up the beach made that an impossibility, so I just watched from the window. I was almost mesmerised by the scene, but curiosity is a powerful force. I was mystified as to what they were discussing, but unsure whether it was any of my business anyway. I wasn't bold enough to casually walk down to the beach and do a bit of public, uninvited, eavesdropping.

The kettle whistled weakly, breaking my train of thought.

Then I smiled. I took a second mug from a hook and made two coffees. Macavity pushed his way between my ankles.

I took the coffee down to the beach. One for Kingy and one for me. Macavity followed like a puppy.

Kingy had his back to me as I made my way to the sandy shore. I heard his words. 'This is a government project on government land. I can't have people wandering all over the island disrupting the project.'

I didn't catch the short, disgruntled reply.

The visitors viewed my unexpected arrival with suspicion and hesitancy. It took Kingy a moment to notice that he had lost their attention. He looked quizzically at them as they watched me carry the mugs to the party.

I nodded a friendly hello to the two men. I got two tentative smiles for my effort. Macavity got an inquiring visual once-over.

'Coffee?' I said to Kingy. 'Anything I can do?'

Kingy looked at me, then back at the two men.

'I think we've said all we need to say for the time being. The rest we can discuss later. Our visitors are just about to leave,' Kingy said pointedly at the men.

The older of the two jerked his head down the beach.

They turned and walked down the beach a short way to where they had dragged their bamboo raft up onto the sand. It was only then that I noticed that the stick the younger man had was really a crude, homemade spear gun.

'Thanks for coming over!' Kingy muttered with more sarcasm than was usual for him. He tugged absent-mindedly at the knot in his red scarf as he muttered something about interfering natives. It was the closest I had heard him make a comment that could be construed as potentially racist.

I looked at him somewhat askance, but he simply took his coffee with a nod of thanks and sat down on the sand. Macavity found shelter under his raised knees. I sat down next to them. A band of storm clouds was forming on the horizon.

We sipped our coffees for a few minutes before I said, 'Well, what was that all about?'

Kingy was quiet for a moment. His anger had subsided, but I wondered when it might again erupt.

A small hermit crab, no bigger than my thumb, was trying to hide under my bare foot. I wriggled my toes and it immediately retreated into its shell.

'It's nothing really, but it can't be ignored. It's as much to do with land as suspicion by some and resentment by others,' he said looking out to sea. 'It won't make sense without some local background.'

He went on to explain that, unlike Australia, most land in the islands was what was loosely termed 'tribal land'. It wasn't actually controlled by the tribes, but by a government body supposedly looking after their traditional interest. Some villagers had difficulty understanding, or accepting this concept.

There was also some freehold land and some government land. The original owners of some of this land had long since disappeared.

'So,' I said, 'there are three types of land ownership. What's the island?'

'It's freehold. Once owned by a German family, I believe, but the Second World War threw a wild card into that pack. Evidently the early Germans, like most colonials, found it pretty easy to trade industrial products for parcels of land.'

'Yeah,' I said with gentle sarcasm, as I sipped my coffee, 'a handful of trinkets or pretty beads.'

'It was often a little more sophisticated than that,' admonished Kingy, with a laugh. 'Often it was tools, axes and even the odd rifle. A rifle certainly gave the owner an advantage in tribal disputes. And of course, western food.'

Kingy went on to explain how the original owners had eventually left and the land lay unused and unoccupied for years. Slowly the local villagers began to assume it was theirs. There was no one around to contest that assumption. No one cared who used the island.

'Then I came along and some little clerk in an office in the capital found it again. They turned the island over to the project and advised the villagers that it was out of bounds.'

'How did they take that?' I asked.

'Not real happy. Only the older generation could remember something about the history of the island. Not much is recorded out this way. The government, being smart, compensated the locals for their "apparent loss". They still had fishing rights in the water around the island.'

'Seems fair,' I said as I tossed the last of my coffee onto the sand. You have your base. From what you said, the government has an international project in their country. Buka Buka Village has its generous compensation.'

'Most of which is held in trust by the Tribal Land Commission.'

'A-hah,' I said nodding my head knowingly. 'No one can get their money!'

'Guess again and you'll be wrong!'

'You have papers?' I asked.

'I have papers. The government has papers, in some office in the capital. I doubt if the villagers still have papers. They rot if they're not stored properly. I'm sure mine have mildew stains all over them as it is, and I'm reasonably careful.'

I stared at the clouds on the horizon. Thunderheads were developing.

Kingy followed my stare. 'Cumulonimbus thunderclouds,' he said. 'They go as high as twenty ks into the atmosphere. There's a bit more trivia for you.' He laughed with a bit of a snort.

'What can you do?' I asked, getting to my feet. 'Those guys didn't look too excited this morning.'

'Well, right now I'm not going to let it stress me any more than I already am,' Kingy said as he pushed himself abruptly to his feet. 'I need to think about it!'

We headed back to the lab, followed by Macavity. I reflected on Kingy's stress level. Was it rising? I thought about the incident with the silver paper, but now was not the time to bring it up.

Chapter 15

Later that morning Kingy started up his generator. His storage batteries were getting low and he needed to do some work on the Mac. He had a few emails to send— monthly progress reports to his bosses, as well as abridged copies to the people in the capital.

The generator was a bit cantankerous and often didn't start first up. I heard Kingy swear a couple of times before it fired.

When he came in he grumbled, 'It's times like that when a bit of percussive maintenance could help!'

I looked at him.

'A good swift kick up the … gear box!' he laughed.

I had a sudden idea. 'Mind if I send an email?' I asked.

'Missing some of your mates?' he said as he washed his hands in the basin.

I mentally acknowledged the fact but said, 'Like to keep in contact—and show off a bit. Not everyone has their own tropical paradise for a holiday.'

'Go ahead,' he invited, 'you know more about the machine than I do. I've still got to get some notes in order. Be a few minutes.'

I commandeered his computer chair and went to work.

```
To: hturner@emailerl.com
From: king@iserve.com
Subject: Eat Your Heart Out

Hi Holly,

Who won the last soccer match?

Great weather. Great tan. Envious? Back
in a few days. I bet you've done all
your assignments. Swotl!

Just dying for a good cup of coffee.
Save a chair for me at Coffee-Pot Shop.
I'll buy you a cup and tell you all
about the rats!

Eddy

(Servant to the King of Wolfe Island)
```

I was never one for literary masterpieces. I put my email in the SEND LATER folder to go with Kingy's stuff.

I could hear Kingy rattling about in his bedroom and wondered who else I could email.

Just then he came out dragging a small metal chest. It looked a hundred years old.

He opened it in the bright sunlight of the back door. He bent over and searched through the contents until he found what he was after. Then he stood upright and held a large brown folder above his head. He could have been the captain of a soccer team winning the World Cup.

'Here are the documents we want! These are the papers we need to demonstrate the legality of our presence here. Not that we should need to, mind you!' He started flipping through the aged sheets of off-colour paper. 'Land agreement, permission to work, residency papers, government contract. All here. All we need.' He beamed with pleasure—or it might have been a smirk.

I noticed that I had suddenly become elevated to a higher status in the organisation. 'We?' I wanted to ask.

He dropped the folder onto the kitchen table and pushed the trunk back into the bedroom. I heard it being forced under his bed. I wondered if he was using some 'percussive maintenance' strategies.

Swinging gently on the chair I again noticed the empty glass with its film of white sediment.

When Kingy sat down at the kitchen table to check his papers, I called out as casually as I could, 'You have another headache last night?'

'What?' he said without looking up.

I repeated the question.

This time he said, 'No. Why?'

I picked the glass up and studied the residue. 'Just that there's a glass beside the Mac.'

'I always have a glass of water there when I'm working.' He sounded a little irritated.

I pouted, knowing he couldn't see me. I studied the glass

again. There was definitely powdery residue around the base. I couldn't tell what it was.

Putting my finger in the glass I wiped off some of the residue. Then I smelled my finger. I couldn't smell a thing. I didn't really know what I was supposed to smell anyway.

I stood up and took the glass to the kitchen sink to rinse it out. I couldn't have Kingy drinking out of a dirty glass!

Kingy looked up without noticing what I was doing. 'Think we'll take a little trip. Let's visit the friendly folk at Buka Buka!'

He shut the folder with a sense of satisfaction.

I looked at him and nodded. I pushed the business with the silver paper to the back of my mind. The subject of the pills was a bit delicate.

Late that afternoon it got dark and the heavens opened up. Rain literally fell out of the sky in great sheets. There was no wind, just a heavy downpour. It flooded the meagre guttering and cascaded onto the ground around the hut like a waterfall. The noise on the corrugated roof put paid to any conversation.

I checked the rats. They were fidgety but not distressed.

Later Kingy and I stood at an open shutter and watched the drenching of the island. As we watched, large puddles were forming on the sandy soil. For the moment I was content to silently enjoy the cooler conditions and the fresh smell of the washed vegetation.

Tomorrow would be another adventure.

Chapter 16

The next morning was humid as Kingy and I set off early for Buka Buka Village, Kingy leading and me more or less tagging along.

We used Kingy's boat to cross the lagoon, then sat in the shade of a rain tree to wait for the bus or someone willing to give us a ride.

After half an hour I grumbled, 'Hope you got the day right!'

He slapped his forehead in mock dismay. 'It is Thursday, isn't it?'

'Wednesday!' I corrected.

'Oh, thank God for that! There's no bus on Thursday!' he laughed. He looked at his watch. 'Unless it's gone it should be along in about half an hour!'

The bus came down the road about three-quarters of an hour later.

'Not bad,' said Kingy. He nodded his head with satisfaction as we climbed on board before the dust settled, but I could sense that his mood was changing. He was becoming more introspective. It was nothing obvious, just that he was a little less out-going.

The trip to the Buka Buka Village turn-off was short, but much too far to walk under such humid conditions.

After alighting, we headed down the puddle-studded track, Kingy swinging his documents in a plastic shopping bag. We both carried a bottle of water.

The village was a bit of a surprise. All of a sudden the jungle thinned out and there it was. It was on a long narrow peninsula with good views of the sea on three sides.

There was quite a collection of houses, but there seemed to be no order in their location. There were no streets. Some houses were close together. Others were set some distance from their nearest neighbour.

Most places were made of timber, and corrugated iron had replaced the traditional thatched roof of the tourist brochures. There was an air of orderliness about the whole situation. Paint had been used with discretion.

I could see few formal gardens, but there was an abundance of flowering shrubs —mainly hibiscus.

Sitting on the spine of the ridge at the highest point was a church. I couldn't tell which religion, but that's not too surprising knowing my commitment to such institutions. It was well maintained. It had had a recent coat of paint and the red tin roof was shiny after the previous day's storm.

'Missionaries had a big impact on the islands,' Kingy said in a conspiratorial voice. 'They have a lot to be thanked for!' he added somewhat indignantly.

I didn't see a shop or any building that could have passed as a school.

A group of teenagers playing a type of volleyball on a crude court stopped to watch our arrival. Kingy gave a big wave and the traditional words of greeting. Several waved back shyly.

A group of half-naked children slowly emerged from behind buildings and shrubs. They followed our advance with big brown eyes, most smiling under lowered heads.

Again Kingy gave a generous wave, but I heard him say surreptitiously, 'Should've brought some beads!'

I looked at him askance.

'Just joking,' he said with a mischievous smirk.

We continued into the village. I was starting to feel a little apprehensive. The appearance of some village men carrying long knives was not at all reassuring. The knives were at least a metre long with large, flat blades. I thought I recognised one of them as the older of the pair who had visited Wolfe Island the previous day.

Was this enemy territory? I wondered.

'Do they all carry knives?' I muttered to Kingy as I attempted to fix a friendly smile on my face. 'What if they don't like us?' You can never find a cop around when you want one, I thought.

'Stop panicking. Just the men and children,' Kingy advised with a bit of a sigh as he gave another grand wave. Some of the men responded.

Kingy recognised one of the men in the group and called to him. The man we had seen on the beach hung back.

I was still unsure about our safety.

'Now to see the chief!' Kingy said. 'Please be on your best behaviour.' From that point on I was more or less ignored. Hardly a word was spoken in English.

An elderly man emerged from the group. He was wearing drawstring shorts over which hung a bright blue T-shirt with NYPD in large black letters across the front. He shook hands with Kingy and acknowledged me with a smile and a nod.

After a few words Kingy and I followed the barefoot man into a larger building behind the church and overlooking a large lagoon. We were followed by a small group of villagers.

There seemed to be some kind of ceremony preceding any discussion. As we all sat on the floor a traditional drink in a wooden bowl was passed around. The bowl looked very much like half of the inner shell of a coconut.

Now we really were deep in the heart of enemy territory!

I was reminded of the peace pipe that cowboys and Indians used to share in old western movies. Roy Rogers or John Wayne or that President guy. When the bowl reached me and it was my turn to sip I hesitated. I was almost tempted to raise my hand and say, 'How!' I almost smiled at my private joke.

'Take a sip!' hissed Kingy.

It was the foulest stuff I have ever tasted. It certainly took any smile from my face.

For two hours we went through the process of showing papers, explaining, listening to argument and sipping. The chiefly NYPD person seemed satisfied with proceedings, but I could see that one or two of the lower-ranking men were not so reassured.

At one stage one of the men stood up and started arguing with the chief. Kingy watched and listened intently. I was sure it was the older of the men Kingy had been speaking to on our beach. For a few minutes there was some agitated discussion until the chief got tired of it and put a stop to it.

Shortly after that the meeting came to a close. We were ushered from the building with much friendly ceremony.

When we were sufficiently clear of the village and making our way down the track back to the main road, I asked Kingy what had happened.

'All sorted out,' he said somewhat smugly.

I had a quick precautionary look over my shoulder. We weren't being followed.

'Come on. Give!' I demanded.

In short, the village chief and most of the elders accepted the documents and they agreed that any grievances they had should be taken through the 'proper channels'.

I didn't ask what 'proper channels' were exactly, but I guessed it was something like a letter to some government office in the capital, or a delegation to the local member of parliament.

Later I was to learn that the local member was a 'brother-cousin' to many of the Buka Buka villagers. His loyalties could lie anywhere.

Kingy did admit that a couple of the men were more interested in direct action. I had brief visions of a fleet of war canoes beaching at the island and a swarm of invading warriors with large knives attacking our 'fortifications'.

'What about the guy in the NYPD T-shirt? The boss one?' I almost challenged.

'I say, do you mind,' responded Kingy very pompously. 'We do not refer to the chief as the "boss one".'

'A chief in an NYPD T-shirt?' I shot back.

'Latest thing from the mission second-hand store in town. You really don't think he stole from the New York Police Department?' Kingy looked at me in a very supercilious way, but didn't ease his pace.

I took a couple of quick steps to catch up. I was starting to sweat profusely.

'Where does Chief NYPD stand on the issue?' I asked feeling a sense of frustration.

'Chief NYPD, as you call him, fully understands our situation. I'm sure he will keep the couple of hotheads under control.'

At this point I made another quick check of the track we had travelled, and this time saw that we were being followed. There was a small band of men some distance behind us.

They seemed to have suddenly materialised from nowhere. Most were carrying knives. I told Kingy.

'They're bush knives, or cane cutting knives. They garden with them. They're not used for slaughtering unwelcome visitors,' he stated more abruptly than I expected.

'Pleased to hear it,' I said approvingly, taking another nervous look.

'Unless you upset them!' Kingy added dryly. 'And some of them are easily upset, as you might have noticed.'

Luckily for us and my sense of well being it wasn't long before a government twin-cab came by and gave us a return ride to where our boat was waiting.

Chapter 17

Kingy was in a brighter mood that night. 'One less thing to distract me from work,' he said. 'For the time being, at least.'

Even the possibility that one of the rats appeared to have some sort of malaise didn't upset him too much. I had discovered it on a quick check of the lab.

'All part of the game,' he said philosophically. 'All games have winners and losers,' he added.

Kingy didn't see my briefest of pouts. I wondered about the meeting from which we had recently returned. Were we the winners or the losers in that game?

We celebrated with a meal of warm baked beans, fried banana and mashed sweet potato, and some fresh coconut water. We had a deep and meaningful discussion on the problems of education on a Pacific island where it was very hard to convince many people that study and hard work were the best way to go.

The documents that had been crucial to the day's meeting were pushed to one side of the table as if they had outlived their usefulness. Kingy didn't have the enthusiasm for returning them to their safe storage place right at that moment. It had been a long day, I conceded.

Next day, with a nod of permission from Kingy, I opened up the Mac and checked the email.

There were a couple for Kingy and one from Holly for me. I had to admit I was pleased.

> To: king@iserve.com
> From: hturner@emailerl.com
> Subject: Eddy—the rat man of Wolfe Island
>
> Hello Eddy,
>
> Your team lost! It's time to come home and give some serious attention to things that matter in life—like soccer, and parties.
>
> I bet you're putting together a scientific paper for your doctorate! Swot!
>
> The coffee deal is on. I've put your name on the chair.
>
> See you soon,
>
> Holly T

As I closed my email I noticed that there was one email in the draft folder. I was sure it hadn't been there when I typed mine up.

Without thinking I clicked on it to open. It was only as it opened that I realised I was reading someone else's mail. I hunched my shoulders guiltily.

I was about to quickly close the file when I noticed what it was. It was gibberish.

```
To: EDD Y2isere-con
From: king@iserve.com
Subject: rrast

Hi edy,

Dcg kill you
miy7========================

Exerpinmtg nomore

3EDF N87 ?

fg sdfcfrfc ccvvvbbbbbnn hbmkl'237
```

It looked as if a child had been playing with the machine. There was no way it could be sent.

I looked at the address again and with some anxiety realised I could make sense of some of it.

It looked as though it appeared to be for me! It didn't take too much keyboard knowledge to guess that the '2' was the lower case of '@'. The 'isere-con' was recognisable as 'iserve.com'. 'rrast' could well be 'rats'. The only other word I could get, except from the 'From' title, which may have been automatic, was 'kill'.

I was tempted to delete it but knew it wasn't mine to delete. I quickly closed the file and shut the machine down. It was then I became aware of a vague ache in the pit of my stomach, something like the anxiety one feels before confronting the unknown. Of course, the unknown might be nothing more than something like an exam paper. Some people call it butterflies. At that moment my butterflies felt more like bad-tempered swamp mosquitoes.

Chapter 18

My mosquitoes took a while to settle down that night. My sleep was restless. The gentle roar of the waves on the outer reef seemed too loud.

At one point I woke when something disturbed the rats. I heard a few squeals and wondered if Kingy could have been in the lab, unable to sleep, or maybe checking up on some aspect of his experiments. Then I realised that there were no lights on in the cabin. It was a moonless night and to my tired eyes the place seemed to be in total blackness.

I lay awake listening for more sounds from the lab. I strained to hear any sound. Maybe Macavity had wandered in. But then Macavity had not been too keen on wandering through the lab for quite a while.

I started speculating wildly about the rats before I drifted back to sleep.

In the morning I was awakened by Kingy making coffee.

'Here. Get yourself around this!' he commanded as I yawned and struggled to a sitting position. Macavity pushed his way between my legs.

'Been out on the town?' Kingy asked rhetorically. Then he added, 'I'm going down to the beach. Sit on the sand and enjoy a quiet mug. It's not too crowded this time of the day. You might care to join me before we start work.'

I looked at him with mock disdain, trying to imply that he was being far too middle class, but the idea sounded good and after a quick wash I joined him on the sand at the far end of our little beach.

We sat in silence for a while then I said, 'Rats got a bit restless for a while last night. Don't know what it was.'

'Didn't take much notice. Thought I heard you padding around looking for the john.'

That was a bit of a joke, as the only toilet we had was outside. At least it was the flushable type.

'Not me,' I murmured uneasily. 'Maybe it was the ghosts of the original owners. Think I'll go back and feed the rodents before they start complaining.'

'They always complain,' Kingy laughed. I left Kingy on the beach. Let him enjoy a few moments peace, I thought. I wasn't aware how few those moments would be.

Back at the hut I stepped inside and put my mug down by the sink. It took a few seconds for my eyes to get accustomed to the dimness.

It was quite a shock to see some damp spots across the floor. At first, I had no idea what had caused them. I bent down for a closer look. They were beginning to dry. Looking up at the underside of the roof I strained to see if there was any condensation that could have collected.

Nothing.

Looking closer at the spots I realised that they were more or less in a waving line across the room. More worrying was the fact that each one contained a few grains of sand.

They were footprints. Barefoot footprints. I looked around apprehensively. Then I listened.

For a moment I felt foolish. They were probably Kingy's footprints, made when he went to get water for the coffee.

That idea was quickly rejected. Even if Kingy had left the footprints they would have dried up ages ago. Someone had been in the hut.

They might still be inside!

I quickly and quietly made my way to the lab and peered inside. I was watched silently by a dozen pairs of beady, suspicious eyes.

I checked out the rest of the house, gaining confidence as I went. There was no one inside except me. I sat down at the table with a deep sigh. At least I was safe.

I got another shock when I noticed that Kingy's documents had been removed from the plastic bag and were roughly spread out across one end of the table. I was sure I would have noticed earlier if they been left like that. Someone had been in the hut. I was sure of that.

If someone had said 'boo' at the moment I think I would have hit the roof.

I stood slowly, realising that I hadn't checked the grounds. I went from window to door, scanning the nearby vegetation.

It gave perfect cover for anyone up to no good. I saw nothing except Kingy making his way back from the beach.

He had to be told and I feared that almost as much as having intruders in the cabin.

My fears were well-grounded. Kingy slammed his coffee mug down on the table. It should have smashed into a dozen bits. It was a wonder the handle didn't snap off. For a couple of seconds he looked as if he was about to explode.

Then he did. For a brief moment I wondered what one did for heart attack victims.

He said things I'm sure could have landed him in jail as he stamped around the room in fury. I half expected him to pick things up and fling them through the windows.

He grabbed the documents from the table in a clenched fist. 'What the hell do they want with these?' he demanded. His jaw hardly moved.

A small, grey feather slipped from the papers and drifted to the floor. Kingy didn't see it.

I looked at him and shook my head. 'Who?' I asked with a shrug and a repressed shudder.

He didn't answer. He didn't have to.

Then he began accusing the Buka Buka people of a whole list of transgressions. I'm sure some of them were true but many were wild.

He was silent for a moment, before growling about the Buka Buka people being a bunch of primitive witch doctors. It sounded a little far-fetched to me.

I had this mad urge to say something sarcastic like, 'We should call the NYPD.' My mad urges have got me into strife more than once. Instead I ventured, 'Come on, they can't all be bad?'

He looked at me sideways, as if to say, 'What do you know about it?'

'Witch doctors and voodoo and sorcery and all that stuff are things of the past,' I ventured again, a little more boldly.

'Voodoo's from the West Indies,' he corrected. 'Sorcery is more to do with the rites of witchcraft. Witchcraft usually involves causing harm to other people. Witch doctors, for your information, are alive and well around these remote islands. In some places religion is no more than a veneer to more ancient beliefs.'

Thanks for the history lesson, I thought as he dropped the papers back onto the table. He was calming down but I was still cautious.

'But they can't put spells on … things?' I questioned.

'They think they can and that's all that matters to them. If you believe it, you believe it.'

That sort of surprised me and I had nothing to add. I was out of my depth with the whole situation.

Pulling out a chair, Kingy sat down heavily and wearily, his head bent forward. 'Shit! What a mess!' he groaned.

Without looking up he asked quietly, 'Did they take or touch anything?'

I told him that everything seemed to be in order, but I hadn't looked too closely.

'Check the lab,' he requested. The storm had passed.

Standing in the doorway to the lab I surveyed the room. Everything seemed to be in its usual state of organised chaos.

The rats watched me intently from crouched positions as if they were biding their time, whatever that might mean. It was more worrying than Kingy's short-lived outburst.

There were times when the rats made me feel wary for no real reason at all. I wondered what they could be thinking at this particular point. What they might be planning—if rats ever had plans. What did they make of our behaviour?

It suddenly occurred to me that I'd been silent for longer than expected. I called to Kingy, 'All OK in here! I'll feed them while I'm about it.' I felt sorry for him for reasons I couldn't really articulate.

'Good,' was his almost inaudible reply.

Later that day as I was sitting on my bunk, letting the southeast breeze caress my head, I reflected on Kingy's situation.

I didn't know what to make of it. Was he going mad? There were moments when I reckoned he was close to having a mental breakdown, but then most of the time—in fact, nearly all of the time—he was calmly in control.

I wondered about radiation. Could he have been contaminated from his excursion to the islands to collect the rats? Were the rats contaminated? I didn't like that thought!

I didn't know a lot about radiation. Was that ignorant bliss?

And what about the villagers? Did they object to having a white man running 'secret' experiments on their island? Did they see him as some lone mad scientist or just an outsider?

Then there were the pills. And the isolation. And loneliness. And maybe even a bit of witchcraft thrown in.

And, of course, there were the rats. How much did I really know about them? I had stacks of figures and had seen quite a few reports but was there something else going on unchecked? Or was I letting paranoia creep into my thinking?

Was there a secret fuse burning somewhere, slowly getting shorter while we went about our task in ignorance?

Poor Kingy, I thought.

There were too many variables for me. I looked back out the window to the ocean.

The day was calm. The sky was azure. The tide was out. I decided that the best thing to do was to wade out to the edge of the reef and toss in a line and catch Kingy a coral trout for dinner. Better still, I would catch us each a big coral trout for dinner!

Chapter 19

Shortly after that I had to leave Wolfe Island for the second time. I had to get back to uni and, to use Kingy's terms, the place was more or less ship-shape. I wasn't entirely convinced, but even though Kingy wasn't one hundred per cent, the rats were apparently responding better than they had for some time. Food was being administered with more scientific control and Kingy was getting a handle on his record keeping. Records were systematically kept and filed. As he said, it was just a matter of keeping the place ticking over until he had some definite results for publication.

Even so, I had a deep-down feeling of foreboding that I couldn't ignore.

'Be careful,' was the only advice I could lamely offer. I was starting to feel protective of Kingy. I had a strange sense of being somehow responsible for him.

I had my last cold shower and rowed across the narrow stretch of blue water to catch the bus back to town and then get my tail onto an inter-island ferry and a plane for the home trip.

It was quite a surprise to get an email from Kingy within a fortnight of leaving Wolfe Island.

To: EddyHaite@iserve.com
From: king@iserve.com
Subject: progress report

Hi Eddy,

So many thanks for helping out. You
were a stabilising influence on an
old scientist I sometimes think is
going mad, or troppo. Or looking for
a place to have an accident! I'm back
into my forget mode again. Chief NYPD
(your term!) turned up unexpectedly one
morning and apologised for the intruder
we had. The man was from his village. He
said they were dealing with him in the
traditional village way. Hate to think
what that might be! We celebrated by
sitting on the ground and sipping that
drink you love so much!

Started getting headaches and some
mild abdominal pains and then I find I
misplaced the pills. They can't be far
away.

Lost some more of my info last night—or
was it the night before. Probably didn't
save it properly—the Mac is getting old
and the salt air doesn't help. It was
hours of work! I was more than annoyed!
I think sometimes I'm on the edge of a
breakthrough—or a break down (joke!)

Have to get some plan for eventually
closing the place down. I don't like
the thought of that but I can't release
the rats into the wild. Who knows
what effect that could have on the
environment.

I sens4 that some of the rats are
getting a bit stroppy. There's one that
spens most of his time snarling at any
rats that looks at him and one of the
others is becoming demented I'm sure.
Bit like she has lost the will to do
anything but huddle in a corner and let
the others throw rat abuse at her.

Old Einstein just watches while the
world carries on in its abnormal way.

Souinds like were getting close to feed
time. (Left the fridge half open again
last night. The rats are getting noisy
andd all eyes are on me—I can feel IT.

Kingy

(King of Wolfe Island!)

The guy's spending too much time alone, I thought. It's
getting to him. I wasn't convinced my reasoning was
the total picture. At least the break-in incident had been
sorted out!

I printed the message off and took it down to a coffee shop
to re-read and reconsider. Any excuse for a caffeine shot at
the Coffee Pot!

Holly was sitting by herself with a pile of books and a half-finished carrot juice, so I joined her. I ordered a cappuccino then I told her a bit more about Kingy.

'The ratty professor,' she quipped, 'on Gilligan's Island.'

I gave a toothy smile and showed her the emails. She read them slowly and then said, 'I think the guy's got problems—and it's more than diet.'

'He's a great guy,' I said defensively but she wasn't convinced.

'You're not thinking about going back?' she challenged.

I started to say 'No', but then said, 'Haven't actually given it any real thought.'

'I bet!' she laughed.

I made a steeple with my fingers under my chin. 'Great sunsets,' I said.

Within a week another email arrived.

> To: EddyHaite@iserve.com
> From: king@iserve.com
> Subject:
>
> Eddy,
>
> Still can't finsd my damned pills. Can you send some. I'm not game to leasve the place in case something else goes wrong. Only have asprin in town anyway. No chemist!! Solar sytem is only just managing as I can't seem to start the

genny as q7ickly as I used to. Water
in the fuel—how that got there 1 don't
know. Hasan't rainned. keep leaving
files in od folders and specd half the
day in FIND putting things back into
threr right folder.

Thingsare geetting out of sync.

Is there a God?

Rats are getting ratty. Put a couple
more down fast night. Rats don't believe
in mercy killing I'm sure. Place went
mad as I took the demented ones away.

They knew!!!!

Havetostop eye4sare throbbinfg. Don't
want

to run out of power.

Kingy

(King of Wolfe island!)

A second copy of the email arrived the next day. Was it an
oversight or was it a sign of desperation? A plea for help? I
didn't feel like I could be much help.

The only additional information was a couple of sentences
added in above the original text.

Did I send this or did f not?

> Forget about the pills—I found most of
> them—in the fridge, behind a couple of
> botles I rarely use.

And a brief PS.

> Slippe ddown the back steps last night.
> Somehow a smalibranch had been left
> on the secon dtop step and I came a
> buster. Knockedme silly (dizzy) for a few
> moments. Got a nasty crack on the temple
> but after a bit of rest and bathing
> things improved.

I sat at my desk for ages, putting bits and pieces together. I was coming to the conclusion that Kingy was in some sort of danger—either from himself, his isolation or from his damned rats.

Within two days another email arrived. I was starting to dread checking my email.

> To: EddyHaite@iserve.com
> From: king@iserve.com
> Subject:
>
> Eddy,
>
> Things have gotten suddenly worse. The
> rats never stop[screeching. I'm going
> out of my mind. The computer has slowed
> down so much that I wait for it to catch
> up when I'm typingr!ll!
>
> My head has made little progress—still
> get dizzy spells from the fall. Or is

lack of sleep or lack of food??? Have
no painkillers left. Can't believe I've
taken tghem all.

No game to le4ave the place in cas esome
disaster takes over.

I think I will have to take your advice
and shut the project down befdore I
lose control. Don't like the idea but
there seems no otther solution. I swear
the little buggers are trying to read
what I'm typing. That's how paronboid Im
getting.

I'm going to have to trash all the
files. I feel if the information got
into the wrong hands it could be used
for evil purposes. (That's how paranoid
I am.)

I actually suspect Einstein and your
Rastus are somehow at the bottom of
the problems. In a better lab I could
isolate them—get some second opinions.

Nolt my option right now.

Kingy

I didn't know what to suggest or how to help, but that night
I had visions of Rastus leading some sort of rat rebellion,
and Einstein watching his cohorts from a vantage point.

Kingy had done something to the rats that he hadn't been
able to predict. Or was it the long-term effects of the

radiation? I didn't have any answers, just unanswerable questions.

The final email, with its terrible spelling and its references to stopping the experiments altogether, totally threw me.

I emailed a quick reply, telling Kingy that I had been able to get some leave from uni. I put the plane ticket on my credit card and hoped that when I came home I'd find a loving parent who would help me pay it off.

I was going back to Wolfe Island. Holly had got that one right!

I let her know that I was going. It was a subconscious attempt to take out some sort of insurance, to make sure that someone was looking out for me.

Within a week I was looking at the cabin from the end of the track. I hesitated before moving out into the open. It looked quiet but I was full of apprehension.

A couple of the shutters were down. I had never seen them closed before, even in heavy rain. They didn't appear to be bolted in place and their support sticks were lying on the ground as if they had been tossed aside.

I felt an ache in the pit of my stomach.

Chapter 20

I cautiously made my way across the open space to the cabin.

'Kingy! Kingy!' I called tentatively. 'Anyone home?' I wasn't feeling very original.

No reply.

It was a bad sign. Kingy rarely went too far from his lab and his all-consuming work.

I reached the back door. It was ajar. I listened for a moment, then called with more gusto than I felt, 'Hey Kingy, it's me. You can come out now or I'll come in and get you!'

No reply.

I pushed the door open. The place smelt musty and dirty.

When I stepped into the cabin it was obvious that Kingy hadn't been there for a while. There were dirty teacups on the sink. Papers had blown from the table and were spread across the floor.

There were rat droppings everywhere.

Suddenly I was worried that Kingy had got sick or had had an accident and left the island. This was immediately followed by a horrible, sinking feeling that maybe his body was lying in a decomposing heap somewhere nearby. I had a mad urge to get out of the place as quickly as possible.

Maybe I should have responded to the first emails faster, more positively. When it comes to hindsight I have 20/20 vision.

I realised that there were no rat noises coming from the lab. The ache in my stomach got worse.

I had an irrational feeling that I was being watched.

I tiptoed to the lab door and pushed it open. I don't know what I expected, but somehow I was convinced that something frightening would happen.

Nothing. No Kingy. No sign of him. Just an insidious smell. More than just the rat droppings that covered the floor. Something was not right! Worse still, there was not a single live rat in any of the cages. There were a few dead ones in the cages, but most of the cages were empty!

'Bloody rats!' I swore—softly.

I remembered the animal I had seen on the shore as I rowed across the lagoon.

I stepped back from the door to get a breath of fresh air and reorganise my thoughts.

I re-entered the room to take stock of what must have happened. There had to be a perfectly simple explanation.

The filing cabinet had been opened and paper removed in a hurry. Spilled files lay strewn about the bench-tops and floor.

The fridge door was wide open. I stooped and looked in. A few spilled bottles of Kingy's concoctions, a half-chewed packet of painkillers and a foul odour.

The oppressive smell of the place was making me feel nauseous. I continued my investigation with my hand partly over my nose.

The computer was still intact, even though the keyboard was covered in rat droppings. Without sitting down I wiped the screen with an old tissue I found in my pocket. The chair looked as if a mad dog had tried to make a meal of it.

I remembered what Kingy had said about rats chewing furniture.

'Of course, if the rat enters a person's house and starts chewing furniture then someone is about to die! That's ratty trivia for you!'

It was a bit too prophetic for my liking.

I hesitated before hitting the power button on the Mac. Amazingly the old Mac hummed and slowly opened up.

The desktop was a mess of files and folders. The trash was full of discarded files. Kingy had said he was going to trash some 'sensitive' files. I had the strange feeling that he had put them in the trash bin but had not emptied the bin. The information was still accessible.

I double clicked the trash bin. Sure enough, it contained a large number of files that looked important, judging from their titles.

I was getting a terrible sinking feeling. I started to fear for my safety.

I went to the email icon and doubled clicked it. There was an unfinished email in the draft box. It was addressed to me!!

I opened it and began reading.

```
To: EddyHaite@iserve.com
From: king@iserv.com
Subject: lastreport

Hi to Eddy,

I think I am to leave. No need to come.

Rayts is gones. I killed them all. Your
are right. Must not worry. All is safe.
The end is
```

The machine died before I could finish reading it. Or maybe the power supply had been cut off.

I hurried to the front door. I had hoped to find Kingy sitting on the steps with a cool drink, telling me everything was all right, but of course he wasn't there.

I looked up and down the beach and gave one last mighty call towards the wilderness. 'Kingy! Kingy!'

There was silence everywhere, except for the waves breaking on the outer reef.

I started to sweat. I felt dirty and grimy, as if I was covered in the smell of dirty rats. I had touched things on which there were rat droppings.

I remembered the well. I could prime the pump and get some fresh dean water. It was a good idea. All I had to do was get some priming water to start the pump. For this purpose there was a small bucket on a rope next to the well. This could be lowered into the well and enough water could be hauled up for priming.

I made my way to the well, stepping over the charcoal remains of a campfire. It wasn't recent—the remains were half covered with windswept sand. Outdoor cooking was not one of Kingy's favourite pastimes, I recalled.

To my surprise the bucket wasn't beside the well. It was actually hanging in the well. It wasn't like Kingy to leave it in the well. I began to haul the bucket up. It was heavier than usual.

As I got it to the top I screamed and let it fall back in. Inside the bucket was the rotting carcase of Macavity. It looked as if the fur had been ripped off his head. I thought I had seen a slash across the side of his neck. I was suddenly sick. I held my stomach while I staggered around retching.

Macavity was not the sort of cat to get into a bucket and then fall into a well.

I leaned against a tree waiting to catch my breath and get my bearings. My eyes were closed tight.

I half remembered an earlier conversation with Kingy about cats and depraved acts. Whoever—or whatever—had done this to Macavity had to be depraved! Barbaric! Macavity hadn't been given much of a chance to use his nine lives.

Slowly I became aware of a sound other than the waves. It was a soft squeaking sound. I thought it was probably birds until it suddenly hit me that it was the sound of rats. My heart skipped a beat.

I turned from the tree and looked towards the beach. There on the beach, coming towards me, were at least fifty rats.

I shook my head to clear it. The rats were slowly advancing in ragged formation. Some of them were really big!

They stopped when I faced them. I felt vulnerable and unprotected. I had awful visions of being eaten alive, bones stripped bare, by a plague of rats.

One rat stood to one side like a military general. I was sure it was Einstein. Three larger rats separated themselves from the crowd. As if on cue, they moved towards me, getting into position to circle me.

I steadied myself, regretting that I hadn't taken my backpack off. I ignored my fear and balanced myself on the balls of my feet.

The three rats had me surrounded, just a couple of metres away. I recognised Rastus. He looked mean and vicious. I was sure his teeth would glint in the sunlight.

They seemed to communicate with soft squeaks for a minute or so. I focused on the three of them, watching for a sudden movement. I couldn't believe how big they were! I don't think they expected me to stand my ground without panicking. My brave stance was purely for show, but it was working. Just.

Suddenly the rat behind me dived for my heels. I managed to side-step and give him a swift kick in the belly as he passed. I thanked God that my soccer skills had not deserted me. The rat snarled viciously at me as he turned.

From the other side Rastus flew at me, snarling like a demented warrior. Again my soccer skills came readily into to play. With a slingshot type manoeuvre I twisted on my left boot and let fly with my right boot. I collected him fairly and squarely. He let out a yelp as he became airborne. He lobbed straight into the well with a terrifying screech.

'Goal!' I muttered softly.

The third rat was about to make his attack when there was a squeal from the pack. Einstein had decided to abort the battle. I doubted that he was about to give up the war. Now that he knew his enemy's potential, he was going to regroup.

As one rat rushed passed me I was able to give it a solid kick to the head. Its neck jerked violently on contact and it was momentarily shaken, but it managed to drag itself to safety.

The last rat made a wide detour around me and scurried back to the mob.

I knew my time on the island was limited.

I hoped that Kingy had somehow managed to escape, but I couldn't be certain. In my opinion he could have been dead. I hate to think how he might have died.

Just to be sure, I hurried back to the cabin looking for some sign, some evidence, that would indicate he had made it to safety, wherever that might have been.

In my disorganised search for clues I looked through the front door to the beach. The number of rats seemed to have increased. Their squealing was getting louder.

I decided not to hang around.

I made a quick exit through the back door and along the track to the boat. As an extra precaution I picked up a large stick. I wasn't going down without a fight.

I found the boat and dragged it into the water. I knew rats could swim but I knew I had the advantage of position and speed. I also had a strong will to survive.

As I got to the channel I took the liberty of having a good look at the shore. Would the rats attempt to cross the current of the channel? I wondered. I would have loved to see them all swept out to sea!

I could see them running around on the beach as if in some state of agitation. Some were actually entering the water. I didn't think they were leaving a sinking ship. They had another motive, but at this stage I was getting well beyond their reach.

I dipped the oar into the water, about to start pulling again when I looked down. There, caught in a piece of old white coral, in less than one metre of clear water, was Kingy's red scarf. It was swirling gently in the slow-moving current.

I remembered Kingy saying that rats contain the souls of old men and should be respected, but I couldn't bring myself to respect those creatures.

On the other shore I dragged the boat just a little way up onto the beach. It would probably float away with the next high tide. I didn't care!

I wasn't going to wait for the bus. I started walking back towards town. An old log truck came by almost immediately. I managed to stop it and get a ride, even though I had to sit on the back with the logs and the dust.

As we crossed the little wooden bridge I didn't bother to look back towards Wolfe Island. To me it was now Rats' Island and I was glad to be well rid of it!

I touched the pocket of my denim jacket. The email that had brought me on this third and final trip was still there. It didn't take an Einstein to guess who—or what—had sent it.

I had a feeling I'd be hearing more of the rats of Wolfe Island. It wasn't a reassuring thought.

.